Advance praise for *Hotel Juárez: St* ...Loops

"Chacón masterfully crafts tales and loops that feel local and international all at once, where the tensions and negotiations of space and relationships on the Texas-Mexico border are alive and electric. This is one of our finest storytellers brilliantly stretching the boundaries—truly a magical ride."
—Lee Herrick, author of *Gardening Secrets of the Dead*

"So many of Chacón's scenes are like images taken by a skilled photographer . . . This is his most ambitious, thoughtful and beautiful book. Chacón takes risks that are both aesthetically successful and emotionally rewarding. His language is disciplined, pure, profound. It is a joy to read a writer who has learned to be so brave on the page. This is a book I will read and reread for many years to come. Daniel Chacón has reminded me, to use his own words: 'A book can whisper at you, call you from the shelves. Sometimes a book can find *you*. Seek *you* out and ask *you* to come and play.' Oh, but these stories are so much more than play. This is serious business."
—Benjamin Alire Saenz, author of
Aristotle and Dante Discover the Secrets of the Universe

"Like fictional spheres created by Italo Calvino, Aimee Bender and George Saunders, Daniel Chacón's *Hotel Juárez* embarks on an unforgettable excursion into fabulous and fabulist worlds, where sentient and nuanced characters often find themselves out of place and out of time, intermittently gazing back at troubling shadows from the past while looking forward into the terrible beauty of the future."
—Lorraine López, author of *The Gifted Gabaldón Sisters*

"Though this magical, funny, occasionally nightmarish book is part of the lush and flowering tree of Latin American political fiction, its exquisite intelligence and fabulism is wholly Chicano. For the risks he takes and the great, unnamed war he's documenting, Chacón has no peer in contemporary American letters. In all its disparate beauties and sorrows, *Hotel Juárez* is his *Guernica*."
—Tony D'Souza, author of *Whiteman*

"Daniel Chacón's *Hotel Juárez: Stories, Rooms and Loops* is a profoundly necessary collection of stories. He brings to life—in extraordinary, compelling and exquisite writing—the violence and beauty of the 'border.' In these brief and powerful *rooms* and *loops* he takes us into an extraterritorial region of self and other, and his stories help us to confront the human heart in ways 500-page novels barely begin to do. There's great mastery and accomplishment in Daniel's writing, and if you are like me, you'll find it difficult to checkout of the *Hotel Juárez*."
—Fred Arroyo, author of *Western Avenue and Other Fictions*

HOTEL JUÁREZ

Stories, Rooms and Loops

Daniel Chacón

Arte Público Press
Houston, Texas

For those who still believe

Hotel Juárez is made possible through a grant from the City of Houston through the Houston Arts Alliance.

Recovering the past, creating the future

Arte Público Press
University of Houston
4902 Gulf Fwy, Bldg 19, Rm 100
Houston, Texas 77204-2004

Cover design by Mora Des¡gn
Cover photo by Daniel Chacón

♾ The paper used in this publication meets the requirements of the American National Standard for Information Sciences—Permanence of Paper for Printed Library Materials, ANSI Z39.48-1984.

13 14 15 16 17 18 19 20   10 9 8 7 6 5 4 3 2 1

The Order of Things

"... esas visiones son minuciosas."
—J.L. Borges

Part I

The Purple Crayon

Broca's Area	3
Between the Trees	9
Camera Obscura	11
Tasty Chicken	12
Cherry Auction	14
The First Cold	20
Cats	23
Dog	24
Birds	25
The New Math	30

Part II

Mais, Je Suis Chicano!

An American in Spite of Himself   35
Dallas Cowboy   38
Green-eyed Girl on the Cover of *National Geographic*   41
How Observation Changes the Phenomenon   44
The Story of Tender   49
¡Centinela! ¡Centinela! What of the Night?   53
The Most Beautiful Book   58

Part III

Juárez Is Burning

Clairaudience	67
Sábado Gigante	84
Exegesis	90
Leeky's Birthday	95
Mujeres Matadas	98

Part IV

The The

The Michael Carver   121
The Framer's Apprentice   130
The First Time He Heard Her Giggle   136
The Spiders (a koan . . . kind of)   142
The Puppy   147
The Things   155
The Lady in the Plaza   161

Part V

Hotel Juárez

Avenida Juárez   171
16 de Septiembre   173
The Best Tortas, Ever!   175
14   177
Piedra   181
Hollister 22   184
3 Stupid Dogs   187
Let the Dead Bury the Dead   190
Poet Warrior of the Night   193
322   195

Part I

The Purple Crayon

"Some called them 'turgid and confused,' while others claimed they were incomparable masterpieces."
Douglas R. Hofstader on Bach

Broca's Area

The baby's first word was *water,* which at first he pronounced as *ahh-eh,* and it was the babysitter who heard it. She thought he had said Papa.

She said, Oh, how cute, and, Too bad your daddy's not here, but later it was clear what he was saying.

Water.

He said it over and over until he got good at it, from *ah-er* to *ah-tur* to water, water, water. The babysitter thought that maybe the child was always thirsty, so she would fill his bottle with water, but he never wanted to drink, he just wanted to say water, although he pronounced it not like *water,* with the stressed syllable on the *Wa,* but wa*Ter,* with the stress on the *Ter.*

His next word was snake.

The babysitter was curled up on the couch looking out the window past the store homes of Kern Place at the mountain up the street and imagining on the other side a hundred blocks of rooftops, past Fort Bliss, where she lived in a hot apartment with her mother and her three brothers. She was just thinking of whatever dropped into her head, and she heard the baby say *snake.*

She thought he was saying cake or lake, and she pictured a cake by itself in the rain, the icing running down the sides like a clown crying in his own make-up.

The baby kept saying it over and over again, until it became very clear that he was not saying cake, he was saying snake.

Then he would say water and then he would say snake and then he would say water snake.

Did they hang from trees and fall into your bathing suit as you walked by? Did they live underneath the shadows of rocks in the shallow part of the water, waiting for your ankles?

One time, as the baby played with plastic colored blocks on the floor, the babysitter was taking a bubble bath. He tossed a block inside the water, and her reflex shifted her weight in the bathtub. She created an air pocket that popped underneath her thighs, and she felt something slivering down there, so she stood up and screamed.

The baby, looking at her dripping body, screamed, *Water snake!*

She stepped out of the tub and grabbed a towel. She wiped the fabric across her back and front, but she was too spooked to finish, so still wet, she threw the towel on the floor and took the man's robe from a peg and wrapped herself in its musky fluff.

The next word was gate.

He said it perfectly the first time, gate, and then he said it again, gate.

He repeated it over and over again—gate gate gate— at the exact moment when she was looking out the bedroom window onto the backyard and the lawn and past the pool to the *gate!*

And he said gate gate gate.

4

And, sitting in his crib under a spinning mobile of butterflies and birds, he slapped his hands up and down and said, gate gate gate gate.

He giggled and said gate and then he put his fist in his mouth.

She backed away from the boy, and she sat on the bed. Then she squirmed her fully clothed body underneath the sheets and scooted onto the woman's side. Maybe the baby could see into other worlds, places that she could never see but that always glowed on the horizons of her imagination, or maybe the baby could hear the voice of God, and maybe the baby, sitting on the blanket with his blocks, was a messenger of God. What words might He write out to her? She remembered when she was a little girl and her mother was *slain* by the Holy Spirit, how she dropped to the floor, and all the parishioners swarmed around her and put their hands on her fallen body and screamed out in terrible tongues. From inside the sheets, she peered across the bed and saw the blocks the boy had arranged in front of him. The letters seemed to be randomly placed into RFHU.

If it were a word, how would you pronounce it?

Roofoo?

Maybe the baby was trying to tell her something.

Roofoo.

For days and days of babysitting, she thought about water snake and gate and roofoo, and one night, when she couldn't sleep but the baby could, she remembered what she had seen in the house's backyard.

It was a nice yard, like she had only ever seen on TV, with a perfect green lawn and rosebushes, a swimming pool, a pool deck with chairs and tables. But at the far end of the yard, there was a gate, an old wooden gate that seemed to be out of place. It stood alone, the wood splintering, as if it had been there longer than the house. Maybe, generations ago, when the city hadn't yet reached these suburbs where the baby's family now lived, it was a gate that led into a dry field with horses and cactus shaded by the mountain. It could have been standing there for a hundred years, splintering in the sun, or frozen under the snow, wet with rain, but now it led to nothing. There was no fence. It was a gateless gate.

And it stood commemoratively in the backyard of this modern home.

Why?

She got up out of those white sheets she always missed when she slept at home, and she wrapped the cool silk around her body and got the flashlight from the nightstand on his side of the bed. She walked down the hallway like a shadow.

She walked past the pool (with the lights on it looked like it had swallowed the moon), and she carefully approached the gate like it was an altar erected by some past civilization. The blue light from the pool glowed on the wood.

She shined the flashlight on the feet of the gate. She was looking for some sign, some mark, some message. That was when she saw what had been carved into the wood.

Wanda and Jimmy, inside of a heart.

Wanda and Jimmy, she thought. Who are/were Wanda and Jimmy?

The baby's parents, Mr. and Mrs. Huerta, were Mexicans from Juárez, a wealthy couple who bought a house on this side of the border when the violence from the drug war got too bad. The woman, who was a blonde and athletic and had green eyes, drove an Escalade with bullet-proof glass, and they spoke English with an accent, and although the babysitter didn't know their first names, because she always called them Mr. and Mrs. Huerta, she was almost certain that they weren't called Jimmy and Wanda.

For days and nights and then weeks and a month and a half, she wondered how all these clues could be connected. What could the baby-god or the god-baby be trying to tell her? It crossed her mind more than a few times that the child could be working for the other side, an evil baby, but with those thoughts even bathing the naked boy in the sink felt icky, his wet skin in her pale pink palms, slippery like a water snake.

The next word wasn't really a word.

He said it right to her, when she was on the couch watching some HD movie on the Huerta's big screen TV about a girl and a boy and a moon and a pickup truck parked on a bridge over a river.

The child started making baby sounds.

She turned down the volume and got up. On the floor, she got on all fours and made sounds the child liked. He was on his back and she pulled up his shirt and blew a wet one on his belly, and that made him giggle with delight. She did it again and again and the child loved it. He said, *Take care, oh.*

She sat up. She could tell he was talking directly to her, looking at her from his play spot on the floor.

He said it again. Take care, oh!

Take care? Was it a warning?

She got up, she looked out the window, and that was when she saw them outside.

She could barely see their silhouettes behind the glare and shine of the windshield where the full moon was reflected. They looked like a four-armed creature.

She left the baby on the floor and sneaked out the back door. She slipped around the side of the house, past the garden hose curled up and hanging on the wall.

She reached the fence and peeked through the slats of wood.

The windows were slightly down, and they were kissing.

He had his hands on her breasts and he was kissing her all over the neck. Then Mrs. Huerta maneuvered herself in such a way that she was a on top of him, facing him, kissing him, and both of them were moaning,

¡Ay, mi amor! words the girl didn't understand. ¡Mi vida! ¡Te quiero!

The babysitter, embarrassed and feeling guilty for having seen it, tiptoed back into the house, across the cold kitchen tile and back into the family room. The baby was lying on the blanket on his back playing with a little stuffed llama and making saliva sounds. When she sat on the couch and picked up the remote control, he stopped playing. He looked up at her and said the next new words. It sounded like, Tennis Steeple.

Between the Trees

The man picked up a stick and stuck the pointed end into the mud and drew an image of his lover's face. It must not have been that good, because when he pointed at the indentions in the dirt, the curves, the round dish-shape that looked a little (he thought) like the shape of her skull, and then pointed at her, she didn't understand. She stared at it, and he kept pointing at it and then at her and nodding his head as if to say they were the same, but she shrugged her shoulders. She didn't understand. She took some of the dirt on the tips of her fingers and tasted it, and then she spit it out.

It wasn't until much later, equipped with language, that he stuck a pen into a bottle of ink and wrote the second draft. His lover, standing near the doorway, was pouring a cup of steaming water. The sun slanted through the window and lit her up. She wore a red robe, and her lips concentrated on pouring the hot water into a clay cup.

He was so moved by her image—and peach trees outside, pink flowers newly blooming, and he could smell them.

He wrote about *her*, trying to capture *her*.

The second draft turned out to be nothing like he had set out to achieve.

Somehow the peach tree pushed her from the center frame of his syntax, so that she was only a small dot on the bottom corner of the page. When he read it aloud to her, she recognized the peach tree and the smells, because he merely said the words "smelled like," but she had no idea what that dark dot at the bottom corner of the page was supposed to be.

Later, he hired actors to say words on stage, and they wore masks that expressed the emotions that, to him, made his lover so beautiful. For the first time he added drama, that is, a story, but the real reason for the work was the beauty of her face. It would be delivered through a tale, a face that could launch a thousand ideas. The story was an excuse for the image. Her spirit was in the language, sliding in and out of the curve of words, her sex wetting every sentence, tingling the curve of every comma, or so he wanted to believe.

He thought he had captured her in the golden cage of his poetry, but after the play was over and the people went home and masks and swords were hung in dark closets where moonlight leaked in from the beamed roofs, she sat waiting for him in the theater. He stood on the stage and held out his arms like a tree and said, Well? What did you think?

Nice, she said, but it was clear she didn't recognize herself.

Then *she* picked up a pen, and as he tried to capture her, she tried too, and they were on opposite sides of the house, both writing about her, and while he continued to write about the color of her eyes, she found that she was able to discover parts of herself that had been hidden away. When she read her first draft aloud, her voice cracking with emotion, he recognized her immediately.

He built a pyre between two tree trunks, and he burnt all of his life's work, every page, every image, every idea. They both watched the flames, felt the warmth on their faces. They saw the moon turn red behind the smoke.

Camera Obscura

When my father shot us, he used a Leica 50mm, 36 exposures, which he developed in the darkroom he had built in our garage.

I remember the vinegar-like smell of the chemicals, and how my father reached up in the glowing blue dark and clamped the dripping photo paper onto the twine. He stepped back, grasped the back of my neck with his damp fingers, and we watched as the square, white face of paper slowly dripped into images we knew, Droopy chained to a tree in our backyard, my mother crying in a thin dress, my sister raising a butcher knife and pretending to stab at the dead.

Tasty Chicken

I'm not a timid girl. You should know that about me. I can be pretty bold; just ask my friends, they think I'm crazy. Last semester I dyed my hair purple, for like a month, and this year I'm thinking of getting a nose ring or a tattoo. I'd like to have one on my hipbone, right here, a moon or a sun or a pentagram or something. I'm not into Satan worshiping or anything like that, I just like the way it looks, it's . . . you know, it's fearful symmetry. I don't think I'd want a crucifix, because it's too conventional, and that's not me. I want to be free. You know what I mean?

The first time you saw me at the Cherry Auction, I'm sure you didn't think, "Oh, there's a nice, traditional Mexican girl I can get to know."

I know it sounds bad, but I don't want to be like my abuela. She still wears those old house dresses with the pockets on the side like all those old Mexican women. That's not me. I can wear anything I want, pants, dresses, whatever I feel like.

Except for one thing. And this is what I wanted to tell you about, so you know, okay? This is why I'm telling you all this.

There's one thing I won't wear, but it's not because I'm against it or anything.

It scares me. That's why. To even think about it gives me goose bumps.

You have to promise not to laugh or tell anyone, but I think you should know if you and I are going to, you know, be together.

You know that glitter that girls put on their cleavage when they wear low-cut blouses?

You've seen that glitter I'm talking about?

I like the way it looks. I really do, but I'm too afraid to put in on my body. I'm scared of it. I know it sounds stupid, and I'm not a dumb girl. I get all As and I plan to go to college.

It's just that I'm afraid those tiny flakes of glitter will find their way into my skin and into my pores. I'm afraid they'll bore deep inside of my flesh and they'll get in there and stay forever like one-celled amoebas swimming around inside of me, getting into my blood stream and reproducing more and more until they take over and one day a giant insect bursts out of my stomach and eats up all my guts and sucks on my bones like I was some tasty chicken.

Cherry Auction

The first time it happened we were hanging out on the freeway overpass, watching the cars below shooting by like billiard balls. José was telling us what kind of car he wanted, trying to give us a verbal picture of it, but his English was so bad he couldn't describe it very well. He kept saying, with his strong Mexican accent, "You know what I mean? Come on! You know that car with the chingadera? That thing, you know. Like a tiburón."

I pulled a pencil and notepad out of my backpack.

I drew the car.

"It looks like this," I said.

Paco and José watched as I drew it. And there it was, the car José wanted, which I knew was a BMW.

"Oh, yeah!" Paco said. "You're right, they're baaad! You can be a beaner in a Beamer."

"¡Qué suave!" José said, looking at my drawing. "How did you do that?"

"It's easy," I said, "It's just line and curve."

"Can you draw a Hummer?" asked Paco. "That's what I want."

I closed my eyes and looked into my mind at the Hummer within. Then I opened them and reproduced the angles and curves and lines that made the shape. I showed it to my friends.

"That's it!" said Paco.

"Man, you're good at that," said José.

"But that's not the kind of car you're going to drive, Paco," I said. "You're going to drive something like this." I closed my eyes and pictured a beat-up Hyundai, and I reduced it to curve and line. Then I opened my eyes and drew it. José laughed and Paco said, "Aw, that's messed up!"

"I'm just messing with you. This is what you'll drive." This time I knew I didn't have to close my eyes to deconstruct the image into forms, I just drew it. A big, mean limousine with tinted windows, and I slid the pad to the gaze of my friends.

"Damn straight!" Paco said.

"¡Qué suave!" José said.

"What about a ruca?" asked Paco. "Got to have a ruca with a ride like that."

I hadn't ever thought about drawing a ruca, so I closed my eyes and in my mind I saw a girl, a cartoonish lowrider babe in short shorts and a tight shirt—her boobs spilling out.

But an image of a real girl flashed in my mind, and when that image transposed over the cartoon image, it didn't fit. It wasn't right. I felt this emptiness —real quick—because I knew that I couldn't draw her. I tried to picture the lowrider babe again, and I started to sketch.

I made her a cartoon with exaggerated womanly curves.

My first lowrider babe.

"Well," I said, showing them the drawing, "in real life she's a lot better than this."

"She's fine," said Paco.

Something disturbed me about the image, and after that day I became obsessed with drawing people.

I was sitting at the Cherry Auction one Saturday morning when I started drawing a woman standing in line at the churro stand. It was cool that day, and she had a knit sweater and a scarf, and matching knit mittens. I continued to draw her, even after she had left, and the woman on my sketchpad became real. I drew a ponytail and gave her a birthmark on her upper lip. It felt good. It felt like I was releasing a soul. She wasn't a cartoon. She was a real soul that was released into my drawing, a real angel from the head of my pen.

I started drawing people everywhere I went, kids playing in the street, old people sitting on the bus, my mom at the kitchen table studying for a test. Then I started painting. The art room at school had free hours when you could come in and use their stuff. I painted in acrylics. At first, I was doing trite Chicano images. I drew sexy Aztec women in the arms of movie-star-handsome Aztec men. I painted lowriders and buxom Chicanas standing next to the cars with short shorts. The paintings were pretty stupid, but my friends liked them and hung them on their walls. "You could sell your art at the flea market," Paco said.

One night I dreamed I was on the shore of a lake. It was sunny, and the water rippled like shards of a mirror, and that was when I noticed that in each shard of water, in each plate of glass, a face was looking at me, thousands of faces in the lake, all of them looking up at me, hoping that I would draw them, wanting me to release their souls into the work. I woke up at three a.m. and drew as many faces as I could recall from the dream, one after another, until the sun came up and my mom knocked on the door for me to get up for school.

How many angels can fit on the head of a pen? As many as you can draw before the ink runs out.

Then I started to draw things that were more challenging, a face looking in a mirror, school children running to catch a bus, an old man walking home with two plastic grocery bags.

My skill became a game for my friends and me.

We sat around the benches in the schoolyard and José said, "Hermano, I sure could use a taco." I opened my sketchpad and drew him a taco dripping with meat and cheese, and he looked at it and said, "Where's the onions?"

I drew an onion and a knife and a cutting board and slid the pad over to him and said, "Cut them yourself."

"I need a cuete," said Paco, and I drew a handgun, a six-shooter, and he said, "No, vato, I want a Glock," and I drew him a bow and arrow.

"Ah, that's messed up."

"Man, I sure wish we could take a road trip to the beach today," José said, and I drew him an ocean. "With girls," he said, and I drew girls playing volleyball on the beach.

We found out that this was a great way to meet girls. We'd be hanging out at the benches at school and José would say to a girl, "Hey, my friend and I can give you anything you want. Go ahead, name something you've always wanted. We'll get it for you."

And the girl said, "I want a nice house in Kern Place," and I drew her one.

I liked to draw with a gel pen, because of the way it slid across the page.

One girl told us that she wanted money. She looked at her girlfriends and laughed. I drew a box overflowing with money, $100-bills falling out. The girl laughed at it, and one of her friends asked to go next.

A car.

And I created it.

A house.

New shoes.

A stereo with big speakers.

A new dress hanging in an empty closet.

Then one Saturday afternoon, Paco, José and I were hanging out at the Cherry Auction, and I saw this dark-skinned Chicana walk by, eyes brown as walnuts.

She was wearing white pants, which made her skin all the more dark, and her hair was long and straight.

I said, "I want to meet her."

"Meet who?" Paco asked.

I pointed to her. She was walking past the booths and through the crowd.

She swerved in and out of people like a panther.

"Ask her what she wants," I told them. "I want to draw for her."

We followed her through the market. She stopped at the churro booth and waited in line. Paco walked up to her all cool-like, like he wanted to pick her up. She wore a red top. Paco tapped her on the shoulder, and she turned around.

"My homeboy and I are like magic and shit," he said. "We can get you anything you want—poof!—just like that. Go ahead, tell us what you want, anything in the world, and we'll make it appear before your eyes."

"Peace on earth," she said.

"Naw, that's not what we mean," Paco said. "We mean anything *real*, you know? Something real."

"How come peace can't be real?" she asked.

"Choose a *thing*," he said.

"No, no," I said. "She wants peace on earth, I'll give her peace."

I started to move my pen. The drawing turned out to be—and I have no idea why, because I drew guided only by the rhythm of the pen—an image of an open umbrella in the rain, underneath which was a couple, walking together across a freeway overpass. They were pressed so close side-by-side that their silhouettes (which I shaded with the pen) looked like one body, yet you could tell they were two. Behind them, I put trees and rooftops of the city. What surprised me—no, it gave me chills as it was happening—is that somehow in knowing that I wanted to create a feeling (and knowing that I couldn't keep her waiting for too long)—I used simple lines, in a way I had never used before. In order to create buildings, I drew elbows, like the capital letter L, upside down. Inside them, I put tiny dots of ink. In the context of the image-as-a-whole, the simple upside-down L's became the windows in buildings. I had never done this before, but as it was happening, I knew that this place existed somewhere, and these people too. I knew now that I was like Harold with his purple crayon; whatever I drew became real.

When I finished, I looked up and saw her standing there. I handed it to her.

I wanted her to look at the image for a long time, and she looked at it for a long time. Her toes were pointed in.

The First Cold

In his imaginary movies, the boy had several loops going at once, all of them moving toward inevitable Hollywood endings. In one story, he was a Star Trooper in a space ship racing after universal criminals, and in another he was a gang leader, a mix of Al Pacino in the *Godfather* and memories of his own father, a thin cholo with a tattoo teardrop under his eye. And he had other loops as well: He was a secret agent infiltrating his elementary school, where those kindly, sinister beings, the teachers, and the arrogant principal, were running a terrorist training cell, so that everything about the school, the structure of the day, the subjects they taught, were designed to brainwash the kids. In another story, he was leader of the world, a king of sorts, but he was in hiding among regular people, because he wanted to know how they think and live, because he wanted to be a better leader.

And because he lived in his imagination, he could do anything, like time travel. He visited the homes of his ancestors, the Tarahumaras, and sometimes he traveled to the future to visit his great-great grandchildren, who lived in a floating glass dome over an HD forest of waterfalls and mountains.

He had so many loops going at once, randomly returning to each one, that sometimes he got confused about which world he was in, and an anomaly would occur. Thinking he was in his gangster story, he once opened a door, but instead of stepping into the barrio, into his turf, into his territory, he stepped into zero gravity and found himself weightless, floating through the Milky Way, a wet passage of lacteous light. He had no idea where he was, but then he saw, far, far away, a blue planet slowly spinning in space, which he recognized to be Earth. He swam toward it, desperate to reach it.

One day, when he was fantasizing about racing in his rocket through a burning galaxy of supernovas, the boy heard the sound of his mother moving in the hallway. She was pacing again, back and forth with quick, angry steps. He closed his eyes, and in his imagination the thump of her feet on the carpet became swirls of thick paint, red and black, spinning around and around, and he found himself falling into the center of a vortex, his arms and legs stretched out like The Vitruvian Man.

He closed his eyes and hoped that when he was spit onto the other side of the event horizon, he would come back into the future, as an adult, maybe a lawyer, educated and successful, or maybe a college professor, or a physicist, someone important. He wanted to be the father of happy children, and when he reached the future, he would re-appear in his childhood home, behind his mother. He would see her pacing the floor, back and forth, angry, worried, distraught.

He'd say, "Mom?"

She'd turn around and scream, startled to see a strange man in her house.

"Please don't be scared," he'd say. "It's me!" he'd say. "I'm your son from the future. I'm a (enter important position) now. I've come to tell you not to worry. Everything will be fine. Everything will be great."

But when he was spit out onto the other side of the event, he wasn't a successful adult. He was still a kid. It was only three years later, when he was 12 years old, on the afternoon she would kill herself. They were in the county hospital, the hallway smelling of vomit and mayonnaise. She wore a long, red robe, faded in color, dragging on the ground as she paced the dim shadowy hallways. Her face was pale as bone, and her teeth chattered. She held the collar around her neck, shivering, as if suffering the first cold.

Cats

One afternoon in the Botanical Gardens, he opened the book and began to read about the cats. As he entered the landscape of his reading, his own world began to blur, and the shape of the letters jumped from the page onto the ground and swirled around into real cats. They gathered around his feet and rubbed against his ankles.

Others jumped on his bench, climbed onto his lap, but he kept pushing them away and trying to read. He thought they were the stray cats that lived in the gardens, unaware that he was co-creating them. After he read the very last line of the poem, *Etoilent vaguement leurs prunelles mystiques,* he put the book down and saw a galaxy of glittering pupils, hundreds of cat eyes looking at him. He ripped pages from the book and put them on the ground for the cats to eat, and they surrounded the sheets of paper, ripped them apart with little, sharp teeth. Some jumped from his lap, gathered around his ankles, a moving blanket of fur.

Dog

One morning a dog was walking along the street when he saw a puddle wide enough to be a pond. He stopped to drink, but as he looked down in the reflection, he marveled at the bizarre world he saw in the belly of the earth, clouds drifting by, upside-down telephone poles, birds sliding by like fish. He saw his own scraggly face, looking down with awe, and he saw the silhouette of tree trunks, standing behind him like sentinels. He imagined they were giants, yelling, "Come on, boy, jump! We'll catch you."

He pictured himself jumping into their soft branches.

The watery glass exploded with the passing of his body. He felt himself floating in empty space, the water splashing over everything, and he wanted to feel free and weightless, and he would have closed his eyes and believed it, but in each shard of broken water, in each jagged mirror of puddle, he saw his own face looking down, the real dog, still trapped up there.

Birds

"What harbor can receive you more securely than a great library?"
Calvino

To get to the library she had to walk through the free speech area, past a candlelight vigil, through a crowd of mourners for the victims of a hate crime. She needed to gather some print material on the turtles of the Galapagos Islands, because the biology professor required the class to have sources from the library, real books, which she thought a waste of her time. Once inside the labyrinth of old tomes, within that smell, walking down those unending rows of bookshelves taller than her reach, she remembered how when she was a kid, she loved libraries.

Her father used to teach art part-time at the university, and they couldn't afford a babysitter, and her mother was long dead, so he left her at the library during his night classes. She held her father's hand as he led her into the grand entrance. He told her to look around, to listen to the echoes and the murmur of disembodied voices. A book can whisper at you, he said, Call at you from the shelves. Sometimes a book can find *you*. Seek *you* out and ask you to come and play.

He acted as if giving her three hours in the library once a week was like handing her the universe.

Anything can be found here, he told her.

Anything. Anything. Anything.

It all depends on what you look at, what books you pull from the shelves, what magazines and journals you thumb through, what conversations you overhear.

She imagined the books were dead souls that slept between the covers, and all she needed to do was open their front doors and they could step out and tell her things.

Now, a young woman, she walked through the library as if for the first time. She walked through the stacks, past a bunch of book titles, and she recited them aloud, *Native Son, The Long Dream, Helen of the Old House, The Thief of Time.*

She passed *Prosper's Cell, Justinian's Flea, The Devil's Disciples* and *Salonica, City of Ghosts.*

She was supposed to be researching turtles of the Galapagos Islands, but she couldn't resist her desire. She pulled an armful of books off the shelves, and she sat in a quiet corner and started to randomly read passages from different books. Instantly the parallel stories spread a white blanket over her imagination, and she found herself standing in a mansion with white curtains, the French doors open, a breeze coming in, a piano playing in the distance, and a moment later the stars in the cosmos were so bright and with fire, and she could see hidden castles in the darkest valleys of the planets. She was so absorbed in those worlds that she forgot about her own, and by the time she looked up to see where she was, it was past midnight and the overhead florescent lights were flickering on and off, signaling that the library stacks were closing. She didn't want to leave yet, so she went back to the book and found herself falling into a blurry tunnel, falling and falling, until she found herself in some burnt-out tenement. She was hiding from the voices coming up the stairs. She could hear the rumbles of car engines from below, and she smelled the city coming through the broken windows, until finally, she was caught. A boy who worked for the library cleared his throat and said, Miss, you have to go. We're closing.

I'm researching turtles, she said.

Miss, you really have to go, the boy said.

She stood up, stacked the books on a small reading table, and left the library.

But she still needed to research the turtles on the Galapagos Islands, so she came back the next day.

She was on the fourth or fifth floor, and she ran through the stacks, grabbing whatever titles intrigued her: *All That Sunlight, The Search for Delicious.* She grabbed *Unchained Voices, A Wrinkle in Time, O Gentle Death.* She carried them like extra bellies across the floor and set them in a dark corner, and she surrounded herself with the books. She picked one up, read the passage, fell into the world, put it down, grabbed another, entered a passage and walked into that world, too.

She found herself floating into a secret garden walled by a stone fence, into a ballroom with gilded furniture, into a fire around which Kopelis danced like spirits in the flames. She found herself in a battlefield with the dead spread all around, and then she put down that book and picked up another and found herself in a room with coffins and mourners. She remembered that black day, black rain falling like curtains, looking down at her mother's coffin. Look to the north, to the south. Look to the east and west, and all of it, as far as you can see, is your inheritance.

But there was someone standing there, looking at her like she was crazy.

Must be some research paper, he said, shaking his head as if he were glad he didn't have to work so hard.

He was a young black man. She looked around at all the books spread about her feet like underclothes, and she blushed.

It's kind of weird, she said, but if you read them at the same time, they kind of fit together.

He didn't understand, so she told him that she could read a random passage and it seemed to be the continuation of another.

He came closer and sat across from her.

Maybe that's why they call them passages, she said. Every paragraph is like a room or hallway in the same house.

Makes sense, he said. That's how our brains work. Whatever we focus on connects to whatever we focus on next.

No, but it's more than that, she said. They're really connected.

Ideas are birds, he said.

What do you mean?

When you watch a bird fly from a tree to the roof of a house, you make an idea, a connection, a treehouse. That's an idea. It's just how our brains work. And yours, he said, looking down at the pile of books spread around her like a big dress, you obviously got a pretty good brain. I mean, if you can make all those connections.

I guess, she said.

When she would try to recall later, try to remember what it was she did or he did that made it possible, she couldn't remember how they found themselves on the floor reading passages aloud to each other. They marveled how well they fit together, as if they were reading the same book. He read about a woman getting out of a carriage and walking up to an old white house by the sea, and she continued from another book, inside a house, and it was dark and a family sat around a fire and their shadows were projected on the walls like cave drawings. I'm here every night, she said, around this time, if you want to find me.

Right here? he asked.

Among the books, she said.

And the next day he found her when she was wandering through a narrow passage, and they grabbed armfuls of books and took them to a corner on the very top floor, near a window overlooking the city lights. That night, as they leaned in close to each other to read the same book, they found themselves making out like teenagers.

She started laughing in his mouth and had to pull away.

What? he asked.

She reminded him that they didn't even know each other's name. He told her he was Thomas from Chicago's south side. He was twenty years old. She said she was Mari, short for Marianne. She was nineteen, Arab-tino, she told him. Her father was a Chicano artist who studied in Paris, and her mother was a Moroccan woman he had met there. But she's dead now.

They were at it again, kissing like it was prom night. They made out, entered passages, and they made out again. They were in Paris, in ancient Rome, on a Wisconsin farm, in rural California. They were in the backseat of his car, making out. She pulled his T-shirt over his shoulders and he unbuttoned her blouse, but the lights of the library flickered on and off.

She stood up, looked out the window. The candlelight vigil was still going on, the third night of mourning for the victims. She could see hundreds of tiny golden flames moving around below her, like fireflies.

The New Math

I decided to create my own math. I don't mean that I randomly wrote down numbers; I mean, I created new symbols for numbers that existed only in my system. I wrote new things like _____ and _____. Sometimes I sat for hours at the table drawing my new numbers, inventing my new math. As I created numbers, I felt like an ancient soul bending over unrolled parchment, writing calligraphy. I was careful on the curves and lines. My numbers were so precise that a slight variation in length or width could make one number become another, and who knew what power it could release? My entire family could be swallowed by light. My numbers were more terrible than witchcraft.

When my mother asked me what I was doing, I told her that I was doing math homework, and she would smile, like she was proud of me, and then she'd look down on my work, and recognizing that my equations were beyond her grasp, she made the sign of the cross.

Then one day it happened.

I was seven years old. I sat at the kitchen playing math. Angélica was in the kitchen, too, over the sink, making dinner, singing a hymn, her back to me.

And they'll know we are Christians by our love,
By our love.

My dad was still at work, but he would be home soon, and outside, across the street, a neighbor was hammering wood, the rhythmic whacks pounding in time.

I was writing a mathematical equation that was so powerful yet so simple that the energy within it could rival the first explosion in the universe. I wrote it carefully, over and over, knowing that within this equation all things existed, the city in which we lived, the country to which we paid taxes, the universe in which all living energy pulsed, all of it, everything from thin metal washers to oceans, those meaningless masses of water. All things were contained within my equation, could be restrained or released by simple strokes of lead.

I worked and worked until I was able to convert it into a single symbol. I knew the moment when I got it exactly right.

I called it the no-number.

It is written like this:

$$[\qquad\qquad]$$

Part II

Mais, Je Suis Chicano!

"L'Art es long et le Temps est court."
Baudelaire

An American in Spite of Himself

I won't go back there, I tell her.

Wait until after the apocalypse, I say, wait until the streets are empty of people and all that's left are ghostly buildings and empty parks, and then I'll gladly show you around that city. I was there at a time when anti-American attitudes were at their peak, but that's not why I hate it, not because I was an "American" (in spite of myself).

I hate it because I was a brown man, a Chicano living at the edge, on the hill overlooking the city. The streets of my district were beautiful, hilly, flowers and twines growing on the walls of homes, an historical district made famous by great painters. I lived in the building across the courtyard from where Picasso had one of his studios, and every day I would walk by, and because I hated his work back then, I tried to ignore his spirit, the reminder that he was once there, his ghost walking right into me as I walked across the plaza.

With the tourists clicking photos of a window that once framed him as he looked out, and people with their noses in guidebooks, stopping in front of his building and looking up for a while, it was hard to ignore his presence.

Just up the hill, a bit higher, past the cemetery, there was a wall of high-rise tenements, where poor brown and black people lived, an immigrant district where I felt comfortable walking the streets, even at night, like I was back in El Paso. I would have been fine spending my time there, but the stipulation of my scholarship required me to be in the center of the city, in the 6th district, with cobblestone streets and bridges criss-crossing the river and white passenger boats gliding by each other in opposite directions.

Everyday I had to walk into a five-hundred-year-old building and interact with the white elite, who were, quite frankly, liberal racists. I've heard all the clichés about racial tolerance in that city, how Josephine Baker felt so at home there, escaping the bigotry of the US, but I can only sympathize with her for all the stupid questions and comments she must've had to endure, like, "You're not like most negros, are you?" Or "Why do your people have so many kids if they're so poor?"

Whenever I went to an outdoor café, a supermarket, a department store, the police thought I was Lebanese or Moroccan. They followed me into parks, like a small band of soldiers, through narrow streets, and they had me put my hands against the wall as they went through my pockets, took my cigarettes and tore them open, let the tobacco fall through their fingers, looking for little brown pebbles of hash. All I had to do was say something or show them my U.S. passport, and they left me alone, but their disdain for me took on another tone. To them, I wasn't a Chicano, I was an American. They didn't beat me, but they didn't apologize either, they told me to move along, like I was a punk-ass kid getting in their way.

I looked like one of the Arab boys who hung out in a plaza or on a narrow street between two buildings, wearing, like us Chicanos in El Chuco, Tejas, baggy pants and baseball caps pulled backwards. Sometimes one of their cars was parked, the doors open, hip hop music blasting, and they yelled back and forth to each other in a mixture of Arabic and French. I would have hung out with guys like that, if it wasn't for my obligations. I was only going to be there for six months, and I had a lot to do.

Sometimes, on the way home from the school, I'd walk up the stairs from the underground, and I would step up into a small plaza, which was down the street from my apartment. Some of the homeboys who hung out around that metro stop seemed to notice me. They used to watch me walk home, my satchel on my side, and sometimes they halfway nodded to me, as if to say "¡Q-vo!"

"How old were you?" Mari asks.

Twenty, I tell her.

"You were a Chicano back then, weren't you?"

But, I'm still a Chicano, I tell her.

I might have dressed like urban Chicano youth back then, if that's what she means.

I tell her I would walk away from the boys, up the street to the plaza where I lived and where the ghost of Picasso could, at best, bite my fingernails, and as I'm telling her this, as I'm imagining the details, I realize something for the first time.

I tell her what might have taken away a bit of my street cred with those guys was the fact that I was holding my satchel, in which I had my large sketchpad and some pencils and charcoals.

I shake my head.

No, no. I don't ever want to go back there, but when she turns eighteen, I tell her, I'd be glad to send her there, for up to a year.

Dallas Cowboy

And then there was the white boy from the other part of Texas, I say.

He lived in my building. It was so irritating to hear him talk whiny, American English with a Texas twang, standing at his balcony and yelling into the phone. He lived a few floors up, and I was on the ground floor, the *pied à terre*, a tiny room with a toilet behind some curtains, and there was only one sink, a half refrigerator with no freezer, and one cast-iron, black burner that took ten minutes to heat up, an hour to hard-boil an egg. The back door opened onto a "private garden," which is what the ad said, but which turned out to be a slab of cement with a planter hanging on the wall, a clay pot with dead flowers I didn't bother to replace. The space was so tight all I could do was take one step outside, stay standing up, arms wrapped around myself. The apartment only had one window, and it looked out onto the side of the next building, but a few floors up, I could hear the Texan's voice spill down into my window. I knew he had a nicer place than mine, with a balcony and a view of the city. I hated that voice. He walked most places he went, like most of us in the city, but I sometimes saw him walking to the main street and hailing a cab. Who could afford that?

Once, I had seen him at the café at the foot of the building next door, arguing in English to a waiter, because he wanted to buy the cup in which his coffee was served—he wanted one like it. The waiter told him it wasn't for sale. "Bullshit," he said standing up, pulling out his wallet, waving around a fist full of Francs.

This was when the Euro was too new to be common, and everyone still paid with Francs, but we all knew the change was coming, and we all knew that the Francs we held in our wallets were about to be worthless. That's how it looked in the Texan's hands, waving the bills in the waiter's face, worthless, like play money. The waiter walked away.

Whenever I passed the Texan in the building and heard his hearty hello, I nodded, but I didn't want him to hear me talk. One time he yelled to me as he ran up the corkscrew of the wooden stairs, "You an artist?" he asked, indicating my satchel, but I pretended not to hear him. He must've just come back from a run or a workout at the gym, because he had on sweats and Nike shoes and a Dallas Cowboys baseball cap. He stopped on the stairs and really looked down on me, from two floors up, while I searched my pockets for the door key. He said, louder this time, and more obnoxious, like a boss, "I asked, are you an artist. So are you?"

I smiled stupidly, like I didn't understand. I wanted him to think me a Turk, or Lebanese, maybe Moroccan or Tunisian. I didn't want him to know I was from Texas, too, because I didn't want him to think there was camaraderie between us. I didn't want to be his countryman, besides, people in the rest of Texas looked down on El Paso, like it was the armpit of the state.

But if it wasn't for that Texan, I would've left the city after my six months was up, never to return again.

Obviously, that's not what happened. Obviously I would end up living there for another seven years. And in one sense, I owe it all to the Texan.

Green-eyed Girl on the Cover of *National Geographic*

I saw her through the window of the art supply store. She had black hair and dark skin, like mine. I saw that she wore a medallion around her neck, an Aztec calendar, so I assumed she was Mexican. There were some rich Mexicans who lived in the city, not many, but there were some, as well as some immigrants who worked in the back of restaurants or cleaning other people's homes.

I was going in the store to pick up some oils, and when I walked in, I looked around for her and saw her sitting at a desk in the corner, behind the counter. She was bent over account books, near a window, the sun shining on the surface of her desk, on some sort of antique mathematical instrument made of metal spheres. She didn't look up at me, not even once, so after I gave the clerk my order and he disappeared into the back, I walked over to her side of the counter to get her attention.

She was writing columns of numbers and letters, her pencil moving across the page like a sketch artist.

"¿Hablas español?" I asked.

She looked up, her eyes wide with wonder, as if she had just been pulled from another world, and then she said something I couldn't understand, not even the language, but the tone had a slight lilt, as if there were a question mark at the end of it. I think she was still inside her head, numbers must have been floating all around her, like alchemy written in the air. I would never know what she said to me, but I now know that she was speaking Arabic.

"*Desolé. Je ne comprends pas,*" I said.

She put down her pencil.

"You are American," she said in deliberate English. I could hear the traffic from outside, piercing horns and grating engines, and a few voices yelling in English from across the river, which I could see out her window.

"*Je suis mexicain,*" I said. At first, I didn't tell her I was a Chicano, because I wasn't sure she would understand what it meant to be a Chicano. I wasn't sure *I* understood.

"Mexican?" she said. She got a good look at me, first in my eyes, then at the rest of me. I noticed now that her eyes were not brown, but hazel, intense, like that Afghan girl on the cover of *National Geographic*. I don't want to over-think my own details, because an interpretation leads to singularity of meaning, but as I think of those two images now, that is, her hazel eyes and the girl in the famous photo, I see how juxtaposing them got us off to a bad start. I exoticized her for being Arabic as much as she seemed to disdain me for being American.

"*Je suis mexicain,*" I repeated, "*etudiant ici.*"

"So you are from Mexico?" she asked in English.

"*Claro que oui,*" I said.

"*Claro que oui?*" she asked. "What is that?"

"*Une mélange d'espangnol et francais. S'appelle code switching. Et tu? Es-tu Azteca?*"

She didn't look up.

I didn't know how to say medallion in Spanish or French, so I pointed at it. "*Este es el calendario de mi gente. C'est un calandrier de mes gens.*"

"I just like it," she said, in English.

I told her about the Aztecs, the city of Tenochtitlán, of the beautiful floating gardens and Chapultepec Park. I told her of the Spanish invasion of the Americas, how Cortez, the *pinche* European, burned Cuautémoc's feet in hot oil. "Isn't that *muy, pero muy* messed up?" I asked. "*Pinche* Spaniards."

She looked up from her book of numbers, and she asked, "*Moo mess up?*"

"*Je parle Chicano*," I said. "*Muy* messed up *C'est a dire, Quelle dommage.*"

"Explain Chicano," she said.

"Basically, an Indian," I said. "And it's *muy* messed up what those Europeans did to our people." Then I looked around the shop to make sure none of her white colleagues heard. "White people are the same everywhere."

"What makes you not a white person?" she asked.

"Are you kidding? ¡Soy chicano! We Chicanos are like the Palestinians. We're natives in an occupied land."

She slightly nodded her head. "The people will help you at the counter," she said, and then she went back to her accounting books.

At once her concentration on the numbers seemed to form an invisible sphere around her. The world dissolved into numbers and graphs. I didn't exist. I was weightless. A body floating through the cosmos.

The clerk who had been looking for my order came back and told me the price and asked if I wanted anything else.

Without looking back at me, the girl closed her ledgers, stood up and gathered them in her arms, and she walked through the doorway in the back of the shop, into a hallway lined by tubes of paint, her figure vanishing down an endless passage of colorful polka dots.

How Observation Changes the Phenomenon

One afternoon, I was walking with another student, a German named Anton, a sculptor from Berlin. He spoke English, and we were talking about art. I was so involved in our conversation that I didn't realize we were walking along the sidewalk in front of the store where Amelle worked. The boy was much taller than me, and I was explaining a belief that I had held back then, which I owed to my Chicanismo, that art for art's sake was a bourgeois concept, and no matter what the ruling class wanted us to believe, all art was political. It was the burden of the artist to make a statement, I told him, and the stronger the message, the better the art.

My hands moved quickly as I spoke. The German guy was nodding and listening to me, his eyes bright, as if he were learning from me, but then he said something that made me want to punch him.

"I admire your passion," he said.

"Fuck my passion," I said. "That's a condescending way to ignore and negate what I'm saying. It's like you're dismissing my argument as *cute*, as the passion of some angry minority."

"No, no, that's not what I meant," he said.

I turned around and saw Amelle framed in the shop window. She stood with another Arabic girl, shorter than her, and they were talking, facing each other. Amelle looked out at me, and she smiled, but I tried to pretend that I hadn't noticed her. She whispered something to the girl, and they kept looking at us.

And, knowing we were being watched, I became even more theatrical. With much authority, I grabbed the tall German by the elbow and led him away, as my free hand rotated around and around, gesturing to the rhythm of my lecture, arguing basically that the artist is either an enemy of the ruling class or its clown. "What are you?" I asked. "An enemy or a clown? You got to choose."

I imagined her looking out the window at me and Anton, both of us framed as in a painting, me looking up at this tall white guy, telling him a thing or two. They watched us for a long time, until I pretended to notice her, and I nodded, very serious-looking, as if I were too busy to come in and said hello.

The next time I went in, right when I opened the door, she looked up. She half-smiled at me, but it was those eyes. Her skin was so dark in that dimly lit store, but her eyes were bright.

They continued to look at me as I walked up to the counter. They gave me confidence.

"Want to have a coffee?" I asked. She didn't say yes or no, she just stood up.

I followed her down the street to a café facing a small plaza with a church hundreds of years old, tourists walking in and out with cameras and straw hats. A poor woman sat at the entrance steps, hands up for an offering.

Amelle ordered a café au lait and looked off onto the street, peaceful looking, like she was sitting in a garden. That's how I remember it. I tried to speak to her in French, but she kept answering my questions in English, not caring if she misconjugated verbs or misused pronouns. "You are study at L'école des Beaux Arts?"

"I'm studying under Machado," I said.

"Really? You must be very good," she said. "He doesn't take many students these days."

I shrugged my shoulders.

"What's he like?"

"A grumpy old man," I said.

She told me she was from a Moroccan family in Marseilles, but she had been living in the city since she was a little girl.

Then I noticed something about her that I hadn't seen in the dim light of the art supply store. She had a knife scar on her cheek. It was barely visible, but it was definitely a knife scar. I recognized when somebody'd been shanked. As she lifted her cup to take a drink, I stared at the scar, about two inches long, and I sensed that she knew that I was looking at it. I looked away, at the beggar in front of the church.

"Do you still live with your family?" I asked.

"I came here with my father and two sisters, but when I turned seventeen everyone went back home but me."

"Brave girl," I said. "Staying in the city by yourself."

"I never did say I was by myself."

She looked away, down at my hands, and suddenly she jerked back in her seat. "You must be very proud to be a Christian, yes?" she said to me.

"What do you mean by that?" I asked. Her eyes indicated my hands.

On the flaps of flesh between my thumbs and pointing fingers, I had tiny tattoos, crosses, something a lot of us did in Chuco. The crosses were a sign of our Chicanismo. I tried to explain to her that it wasn't about Christianity, it was about rebellion, about asserting one's culture.

"Yes," she said, "Americans are always *asserting* their culture."

"You don't understand," I said. I held up my hands. "This was adolescent rebellion. This was la vida loca. And I'm not American."

I definitely didn't tell her I was a Texan.

"You speak French like an American," she said, looking away, across the street, at the stone church, at the Arab lady.

"Well, I'm not."

"Do you like living here?" she asked.

"It's all right. A little alienating for a Mexican guy."

She slowly turned around. "A Mexican guy," she said to herself. Then she said to me, "My sisters are here this weekend. Too bad you have no friends here."

"What do you mean?" I asked.

"If you had friends, we could all go out together," she said. "A triple date."

Date, I noted.

"No problem," I said. "I got lots of friends."

"That guy I see you talking with? He's your friend?

"Yeah. He's a German guy."

"Can you get him to come?"

"No problem."

"And one more friend too. But no Americans," she said.

"As far as I know there's only one American in the whole school this year."

I didn't tell her I was him.

"Fine. And don't forget: you told me you are Mexican."

"Puro mexicano," I said, and then I did a little mariachi grito to prove it: "¡Ajúa!"

She actually smiled at that.

The Story of Tender

I needed friends and quick.

I hunted down Anton and asked him if he would like to go out with us. He wore glasses and had pale blue eyes, his face thin. He looked more like a scientist than a sculptor. "I got the impression you didn't like me too much," he said. "After our last conversation."

"Oh, man, we were just talking politics. That's all. This is something altogether different. They're . . . you know? Women. Let's have some fun."

"Well, as you Americans say, Let the good times roll."

"I'm not American," I said. "I'm a Mexican."

"Really? I didn't know that."

The problem was the other guy. I had spent so much time hating everybody, feeling alienated, contributing to my own alienation, that I really hadn't met anyone. I only had one day to find a third person. I went to bars and cafés hoping that I could meet a guy and ask him to go out with us, but it was futile, and I felt ridiculous.

Then one evening, as I walked up the street to home, I saw Mitch, the curly-haired blond Texan in front of the building in the small plaza drinking beer and talking loudly to another boy.

"This place bites," he said. "We should go to Barcelona."

"Is it good there?" asked the other boy, also with a US accent.

Mitch was handsome, like a cologne model.

I stood watching him talk to the other boy, thinking that his looks might forgive his personality. Maybe I could convince him not to open his mouth all night long. Maybe we could say he was from Canada.

"You're an American?" I asked him, walking up to him, and I extended my hand for a firm American shake.

"Damn right I am," he said, grasping my hand.

"Me too," I said, "and a Texan at that."

"No way!" he yelled. "What's your burg?"

"Lubbock," I lied, thinking he might think El Paso wasn't really Texas.

We talked a while, about inane things, and I had one of their Heinekens. After his friend left, it was only Mitch and me standing outside watching people walk through the *place*, that is, the little plaza, watching people stop in front of Picasso's studio to take pictures.

"Here we are," he said, "two Texans in Paris. That's awesome,"

I asked him, "You got plans this weekend?"

"What you got in mind?"

"I know some girls," I said.

"Girls?" he asked, interested.

I told him about Amelle and her sisters, and Mitch asked if they were French girls. "Well, French Moroccan."

"Arabs!" he said, pronouncing it A-*RABS*. "They don't like Americans."

"Say you're Canadian," I said.

And that was how I was able to have a first date with her. We went to a club.

Her younger sister and Anton, the German sculptor, hit it off from the start. They sat in a corner and spoke in French. His French was fluent and natural, and they danced a lot, too. He was tall and skinny and she was short. He was pale, white, and she was dark-skinned, but somehow they looked good together. Her name was Sonia, and she was tiny, even her hands, small enough to belong to a child. She was eighteen.

The older sister, Mitch's date, was twenty-three. She had a rough edge about her, as if she were street smart. Why she put up with Mitch, I don't know, maybe for his looks, maybe for her sister's sake. She dressed flashy, showing a lot of flesh, and she smoked one cigarette after another and drank more than all of us. Once, as we sat around a table, I saw her look at Mitch as if she hated him, puckering her face in disgust, as she blew out her cigarette smoke.

I thought that both sisters were putting up with the other two for my sake, for Amelle's sake. I thought we truly liked each other. She was sweet and funny and had very strong opinions about art. She hated Picasso, and she could go on at length with many reasons why, mostly for his objectification of women. I hated Picasso then, too, but for different reasons, more superficial than hers. He was too popular, so maybe I thought hating him showed how much I rejected popular opinions on art.

We sat at the table talking in English, while her sisters and the boys danced. She seemed reluctant to speak French with me. When the bill came, the others were still on the dance floor, and I looked at it.

It was the first time I could see the future in a bar bill. It had two prices listed, one in Francs and the other in Euros. "Never seen this before," I said.

She grabbed the check and looked at it. "What?"

"It has the price in Euros, too."

She looked at it, shook her head. "Better get rid of our Francs," she said. She opened her purse and pulled out a bunch of bills.

"Let us get it," I said, meaning the boys. I didn't have enough to cover it on my own, and what little cash I had was all I had for the rest of the month.

She kept piling Francs on the table.

I pulled some out of my wallet and we stacked them on the table. Anton saw us from the dance floor, and he wanted to make sure he pitched in, so he threw a pile of paper Francs on the table. Amelle counted it and stacked it into neat piles. We looked at all that paper, knowing how useless it would be in a few years, like the story of tender was about to end.

¡Centinela! ¡Centinela!
What of the Night?

The Latin Americans had brought out DJ equipment and giant speakers and placed them on the bank of the river, in a circular arena made of stone, and they danced. They danced all night long to salsa and cumbia, danced as they lifted wine bottles, even their shadows danced elongated across the surface of the water. They were sexy, the way they moved, like models in a beer commercial, and tourists on the passing boats screamed their approval, taking flash pictures.

Amelle asked me why didn't I talk to some of the other Latinos. "You must have a lot in common with them," she said.

I knew my Spanish wasn't good enough to blend in.

I knew that the moment I tried to speak, they would laugh at my accent, "out me" as an American, so I told her they were bourgeois Latinos, fresas, I said, and I had no desire to be with them.

Truth is, as I heard the music and watched them dance, I wanted so much to be part of them. Amelle's two sisters were dancing, Anton with Sonia, and Mitch and the older sister dancing on one of the stone edges, water on the other side of them like an infinity pool. I wanted to dance like the Latinos, wanted to feel the rhythm electrifying my bones, but I couldn't dance. I was clumsy and awkward.

Amelle looked bored with it all, like she didn't want to dance, didn't even want to watch them dance. She looked at the water, and when she couldn't stay still anymore, she stood up and said, "Come on."

She wanted to walk.

So we walked. We walked across the street and into a neighborhood.

She turned onto the narrowest streets possible, the darkest walk, looking for dark, and we entered into an alley that had an arch at the entrance, lined by the windows of people's homes, silhouettes of solitude standing in the doors of balconies.

At the end of the dark, we saw a glimmering light, and as we curved with the path, we saw an old house in the glare, several stories high, a mansion, but now, it looked like it might have been a museum or a gallery or a community center. On the top three floors, the windows were lit up yellow, sheer white curtains slightly parted, bookshelves in each room.

"Look at all those books," Amelle said, standing still, looking up.

Then we heard glass shattering, and we looked to the entrance of the mansion, and only then did we notice that something was going on inside, the double doors open, the shapes of people moving around, light spilling out onto the street, all the way to our feet.

I never told my daughter this part of the story, because I don't remember what was going on in the house, or where we were exactly, maybe an estate sale, maybe a party, something private that we crashed, maybe something open to the public, an art opening, a reception with cheese and wine and a jazz trio, or maybe a full orchestra, maybe it was a ball. In telling our stories, we have to give up part of our imagination, because if I ever told my daughter about this night, I would have to choose the details to tell it, limit the possibilities.

I remember she walked into the light ahead of me, as if she belonged there, chandelier shining down on that first floor of the house, or the building, or the museum, or the gallery. I remember the floors were shiny, a dance floor, like a room in Versailles, Louis 14th's ballroom, floors smooth as marble, reflective, and I saw me and her down there, inside of the floor. And maybe this is why I never told my daughter this part of the story, because every time I try to recall walking into that light, I somehow remember a few years later, after we would get married and have Mari.

It was afternoon, and we were older then, walking in a park with our little girl in a stroller, and then the lights flashed in the floor and I could see us down there like an amateur movie with too much exposure, Amelle pushing the stroller a few steps ahead of me. She was approaching a pond, where a statue of a nude lady stands in the middle, her palms raised, as if catching raindrops, a sunny day, the nude woman in the middle of the mirror, and suddenly a little arm popped out of the stroller, *boing*, and we heard this little tweet, *Who is she?*

Amelle looked to me, a few steps behind her, wanting me to answer our daughter's question.

Who was the woman in the water?

A ballerina, I said.

I lifted you out of your carriage, and you were all draped in white, white knit cap, white blanket, and without even taking off my shoes, I stepped into the pond and danced with you in my arms, wet to my knees, and you shined with delight.

I know we walked around in there, among the movement of people, like brushing against ghosts, cold drafts of wind passing over our shoulders, the howl of the city coming in from the open doors.

Did we look at paintings? Did we pull tulips of champagne from silver trays held by uniformed waiters? Was it an art showing, and did we walk from frame to frame, painting to painting, looking into the field at an old icehouse, a hollow frame of brick and rubble?

Lights came up on an orchestra, and only then did we notice the orchestra set up on the veranda overlooking the ballroom, violins, violas, pianos, clarinets, flutes. They played a waltz, and people spun onto the floor with big dresses and shiny jewelry, and they danced all around us. I held her waist, took her single hand, and we danced. The light from the chandelier shined on her face, making her skin slightly yellow, and I looked at her face so close I could see goose bumps on her cheek. We were spinning around, I had her hand in mine, her skin was cold, and the lights blurred by her head, and again, it was at this point that lights come up inside the floor of my memory.

We are looking into our first apartment. It's one of those immigrant tenements at the edge of the city. Amelle stands before the window, looking out on to the street. She's angry. I see her shoulders tense. I'm sitting on the sofa. She calls me names, cusses me out in a mixture of French and Arabic. The baby starts crying, so I stand up, and I pick her up, and I hold her in the air and dance with her.

And we were dancing, all three of us, surrounded by the bodies of other people dancing. How many of them that were there that night are now dead, like Amelle, no one can know, but there were some older people there, so the fact is, we were dancing with the dead, and I was dancing with Amelle. I ask her does she remember that day in the park that hasn't happened yet, and she nods her head, and asks, *She wore white that day, didn't she?*

I nod.

She looks away, across the floor of the ballroom, up there where members of the orchestra sit on chairs with instruments. There is a circle of rooms, all the black doors facing the floor, like Solomon's men guarding the palace.

But somehow she knows we're already married, and that what happens next has already happened. And because memory is a dream, every time I think of this, I am dreaming, and she meets me there. Memory is where you can hang out with the dead. We dance, brushing against the other bodies of other people. I touch the scar on her face, my caress a question mark. A blue light flashes beneath our feet, and we look down and see a large man pulling her by the wrist. He is dragging her on the floor and she is screaming, and he stops, and he looks down on her.

She pulls me away to another part of the floor.

What was that? I ask.

Nothing, she says, forget about it. Let's go upstairs.

Upstairs?

Remember those books we saw from the street? she asks.

The Most Beautiful Book

We snuck up there, away from the event and the crowds, running up those stairs and entering the first door we could reach. We didn't think anyone had seen us.

We found ourselves in a room that smelled of old fabric and books. The walls were red with wallpaper, and there was a velvet couch and lots of bookshelves. It looked like one of those antique rooms in the Louvre, and it even had a tapestry hanging from one wall, trees, lush bushes, a river, a white swan, a castle in the distance, mountains. We walked around, holding each other's hands. On the other end of the room was a double door, which opened onto a hallway.

We went down there and into another room, which was also full of books, and the furniture seemed the same style, velvet sofas and skinny lamp tables. We went into room after room and they seemed the same, so we knew we were in someone's private library. Most of the books were in French, and I grabbed one from the shelf.

It was called *Sept ans chez les hommes libres*. I opened and read: "A vous parlez franchement, je mets tous les soldats de tous les pays dans le meme sac! Flanquez un uniforme bleu, jaune, rouge or khaki sur un gars arraché . . ."

She pulled the book away from me and handed me another one, *The Revenge of Prometheus* or something like that, some book in English.

"Read that," she said.

"What for?" I asked, looking for the book that I was reading. "It was getting interesting," I said. "Here's one in Spanish!" I pulled out a book called *Canto cósmico* and read from a random page, "Dos seres se separaron para siempre. No hubo ningún testigo en aquel adiós." I put it down and picked up a French translation of *Crime and Punishment*. "I love this book," I said, but she said, "No," and she took it from me. "Please do not read aloud in French."

"If anyone catches us," I said, "we can say we were just looking for the bathroom."

"That's not why I don't want you to read," she said. "Read in English. That's okay."

She left the room and I followed her into the hallway. The row of lights on the ceiling followed the descent of doors, and following them, I bumped into her. She was staring at the room at the end, standing there frozen, like she had seen the dead.

"Hey, are you all right?" I said, trying to pull her out of the trance.

"Do you know what I just remembered?"

She put her hand over her mouth and looked as if she was about to cry. "Oh, Allah! Do you know what, Victor?"

"What?"

"There was a book I read, when I was a girl."

"What book?"

"I don't remember. I just remember I loved that book."

Her eyes were glassy.

She said it was a book she had found in some library, she couldn't remember where, and she started reading it and it was beautiful.

"What was it about?" I asked.

"I don't remember." She tried recalling, but she couldn't, not even a single detail, not a word. All she could picture was a glow on her arms and face as she read. "I loved that book."

"Well, we're here among a bunch of books. Let's look for it."

"That's crazy," she said. "It's statistically impossible."

"Rarer things have happened."

She went deeper into the hallway, disappearing from my view, and by the time I got near her, I saw her ankle disappear up another set of stairs, into the ceiling. I ran up. Between two bookshelves there was a small, circular window that looked out onto the street. She stopped and looked out. "It's lost forever."

"No it isn't," I said. "Our souls have a way of finding what books we need. You just have to believe."

She rolled her eyes.

"What?"

She turned around to face me, and said—as if she had bad news for me—"How can I say it? You talk like an American. Like you watch too many movies with happy endings."

"So maybe I am influenced by the dominant culture. I told you I was a Chicano."

"What?"

"Maybe this is it!" I thumbed through the pages of a book with illustrations, a rabbit running across a field. "Let me read a passage. See if you recognize it. Wait, I think it's in Latin."

"Explain this," she said.

"Explain what?"

"You told me that a Chicano was a Mexican."

"Well, it's more complicated than that," I said.

"Complicated?"

"Well, we *are* Mexicans. Most of our parents are from Mexico. We are, too, really, from Mexico, but we're also US citizens."

She put her hands over her mouth, and her eyes grew wide. "You are American!"

She said the word *American* as if it could be replaced with *murderer* or *child molester*.

"But, I'm a Chicano," I said. "There's a big difference."

"I knew it," she said. "But you know what?" She walked over to a shelf, and without thinking, she pulled out a book. "Even though you lied to me that is okay." She thumbed through the shadows of the pages. Then she slammed it shut and put it back.

She walked past me, down the hall.

"It's not my fault I was born on the US side of the border," I said to the sound of her leaving, as if trying to get in the last word. "All my gente come from Ciudad Juárez."

She came out of a door and appeared in front of me. "I've known it all along," she said. "It was very interesting to see a liar in action."

"I wasn't really lying," I said. "Not really."

"That is why you will not talk to Latin Americans. They would know you are a liar. No matter," she said, and she kissed me. "I like you."

Then she slipped into another room and said, "See if you can find me."

She was gone.

I tried to follow her.

I entered another room. As I walked, the boards creaked beneath my feet. That's how I remember it.

Outside in the hallway, I saw a shadow slide across the wall. I went out there to look for her, walked down the hall thinking I was following her footfalls, but later I realized that I was following the echo of my own steps. The acoustics of the house somehow fooled me into believing that my echo came first. It was like an Escher house, and going up the stairs I might confront an earlier version of myself going down the stairs. Or maybe I'd confront an earlier version of her, walk into a room and there she was, a little girl, reading the most important book of her life, and maybe, I could walk in on her sometime in the future, that day she would be killed, and I could stop it from happening.

I felt a shadow over my shoulder, and I followed it into the hallway. I had climbed so many stairs that I was certain that I was on the topmost floor, but I found the last stairs, more of a ladder than a staircase, one that had been pulled from the ceiling by a rope.

I climbed up.

There were no windows, and the smell of books was intense, like breathing in dust and words. There were books all around the floor as well, some of them in piles, as if the collectors had carried boxes up there and emptied them onto the ground, and there was a couch.

I stood there, as if in a capsule, and I gazed around at the titles. I tried to read, but they were in a language I didn't understand, a script I didn't recognize. I wasn't even sure how to read the pages, up to down, side to side, left to right, because the written words looked like a bunch of symbols, but as I think of it now, it could have been ancient Hebrew or Aramaic. I saw one book with a letter on the cover that I thought I might have recognized, a character shaped like a candleholder. I pulled it from the shelf, and that was when I found the breach.

As the book came out, light came from the bookshelf, shot into my eyes. The books next to it fell into the spot, and the light went out. I took out another book, and the light flashed in my eyes and went out again.

I realized that the walls of this room were next to the giant chandelier that lit all the way to the bottom floor and out the door, and when I pulled out a book, I could see the light. It felt like I had discovered a breach in the fabric of space.

"I guess I'm pretty easy to find," she said, stepping into the light.

We floated into each other's arms. I smelled the sweat on her neck, the wine on her breath. We kissed. I led her to the couch and sat. She sat on me, facing me, and as stupid as it was for both of us, we used no protection.

Later, we heard footsteps coming up the stairs. We got off the couch, and she went to get dressed in the shadows. I stood up and grabbed a book off the shelf and pretended to be reading. A man's head appeared in the light of the entrance. He was tall. I pretended to be engrossed in the book. I remember seeing her silhouette pulling the blouse down her shoulders, and as the man stepped into the doorframe, standing there like a soldier, she froze like time had stopped.

Part III

Juárez Is Burning

"La cola celeste se empieza a manifestar."
Brujería

Clairaudience

I.

Claire is frozen before the window, in the tableau of a woman brushing her hair, the church bells ringing the noon hour.

I can go either way, I tell her.

I'm really not interested, she says when the church bells stop, and she starts brushing her hair again, long and red. It's full of sun as she brushes it, as if that entitles her.

I don't care what you do, she says.

If it doesn't concern her, it doesn't concern her.

She's been my roommate for three years, and I kind of wish she would move out, but our apartment is beautiful, hardwood floors, high ceilings, a fireplace with a tile mosaic of leaves and flowers. From our living room, out the bay windows, you can see the downtown skyline and a sea of lights behind that, which is Ciudad Juárez. It would look like a big city apartment in a romantic comedy, if the neighborhood wasn't a run-down barrio, east of downtown, where rent is cheap.

Well, she's your girlfriend, I say. You should care about this.

What-evs, Claire says.

II.

My bedroom overlooks the cathedral. My windows are big. I have two of them, side by side, both of them framing the cathedral like a painting, a large and orange dome, and beyond that the endless gray sea of the city. At night the lights are stunning.

I keep the windows up year round, because I want to hear the bells. They ring every hour. I like that they tell me the time, and I even like the little tune they play before they toll the hours, a tune I take to work.

Dum dum da-dum dum.

Dum dum da-dum dum.

Catholic bells a-ringing!

BONG . . .

BONG . . .

III.

I'm not Catholic.

When I was in high school I was a Christian, very evangelical, and we didn't believe that Catholics were saved. That Virgin Mary really bothered us, I think, because she was a woman *and* a deity.

Goddess was just another word for witch.

IV.

The bells piss off Claire. One time she wrote a petition to outlaw the bells, and she went all around the block, but everyone on our block is Mexican, and they're Catholic, and they like the bells, and the only signature she got was from one of the lowriders across the street. He wrote "pinche malinche."

She goes around the apartment cursing and slamming shut the windows, screaming, Always the fucking bells bells bells bells! Bells bells bells bells!

Like a tune she hates.

bells bells bells bells!

bells bells bells bells!

She turns on *All Things Considered*, and she puts it at full volume, but it can't kill the bells. You can feel them even if you can't hear them, because they vibrate on the wooden floors like a tell-tale heart.

Dum dum da-dum dum.

The tune stays with me all day, animates me all day, and at work customers sometimes ask me, What did you say?

Just humming a song, I say.

V.

The new girl pointed at me, and she said, I know that song!

Her name was Aimee Pratt. I gave her a look, like, *Hello? They're bells, not a song,* but she was thinking about it. I imagined her going through her mental iPod looking to name that tune. When the answer came to her, she snapped her fingers, *Frère Jacques!* That French song about the Catholic monk and the bells, right?

VI.

I can hear the future.

Even when I was a little boy.

I knew when a man was going to stick around.

I knew from the first time I heard his voice buzzing from my mom's bedroom, like a horsefly. I could hear everything, not just the noises they were making at the time, but I could hear the future.

I knew by the sound of his laughter when a man would come again and again.

I knew by the sound of his cough when a man would come only once.

I knew by the sound of his questions, the inflection at the end of his sentences (when the question mark comes out of nowhere?) which man would move in for a while, and how long he would stay, and what he would take with him before he left.

I would try to warn my mom when I heard danger, but she thought I was jealous, and that every man she brought into her bed was *The One.*

Even now she lives alone. My old bedroom, filled with two generations of junk, piles of newspaper, chairs stacked against walls, boxes of clothes, smells like old, sweet denim. The entire house is full of dusty things from her past, and her bedroom is the only room she can move around in. It has no windows, but on the other side of the wall, you hear sharp sounds piercing the city.

VII.

By the way Aimee Pratt hummed the Catholic bells
while she wiped the tables, by the way she sang as she
worked as the barista, by the way she winked at me
when she noticed me observing her, I thought she would
stay at the café with us forever. I thought I heard our
future in the song she sang,
   I love coffee!
   I love tea!
   I love the Java jive and it loves me!
   But I was wrong.
   She quit after two weeks.
   But now she's with Claire, me, the unwitting match-
maker. Now we're one big happy family, other than the
fact that Claire hates me.

VIII.

The manager, Julio, hates to hire people. Do this for me, cariño, he asks, and hands me the apps.

Fourteen girls had wanted Aimee's position. I interviewed them all. I had a list of ten questions.

I listened to their answers.

I remember that day like a montage from a comedy movie, a line of different girls sitting across the table from me.

I love people! said a blonde with lots of hair, like she was talking about chocolate.

I need to pay my way through college somehow, don't I? asked a black-haired girl with black make-up.

I mean, you know? she said, like I was an idiot.

Sometimes I wrote things on their applications as they answered a question, something like "okay" or "good answer," and sometimes I forgot to listen to what they were saying and I wrote random things, "empty jewel," "bitter box," "so says the ocean." I could tell when they tried to peek over the desk to see what I was writing.

IX.

When Aimee Pratt walked in, the wind came with her. Her application blew off the desk and I had to go underneath and get it. By the time I stood up again, she had closed the door.

Very windy today, she said, her hair all blown about and wet from rain.

I gestured to the empty seat in front of the desk, and I sat down opposite her.

We were silent as I looked over her application.

So, you're the big cheese, she said, not quite like she was flirting or as if it were a real question, but just as if to say something. I liked the way she said it too. I mean, as if she had confidence and was kind of teasing me.

But I'm not the big cheese.

I'm not even a slice.

Maybe I'm one shred of grated cheddar on the whole enchilada.

X.

Next week is Aimee's birthday, and I haven't decided what to get her.

I've got it narrowed down to two things, and I can go either way.

One is a collection of romantic movies like *When Harry Met Sally* and *Sleepless in Seattle*. The package is called Chick Flick Picks. They send a movie a month.

They're about boy-girl relationships, but Aimee and I like them anyway.

Claire hates them. One time she walked in on us when we were under the blankets on separate sides of the sectional. We were watching a movie starring Matthew McConaughey.

I like him.

Claire was just getting back from work. She's a free-way flier, which means she teaches a dozen classes of freshman composition, driving all day from university to university, from college to college, lugging around stacks of student papers like used phone books.

Aimee and I were almost in tears watching Matthew fall in love.

Claire, standing before the couch, looked down on us, as if she were looking down on us.

It's socialization, she said, heterosexual propaganda. What they don't tell you is what happens after the last kiss. The guy gets tired of her beauty, he belittles her, he convinces himself that he fell out of love with her or that they're growing apart, and then he has another romantic comedy waiting to happen. Besides, half those actors are queens.

It's just for fun, Aimee said, a little irritated at Claire.

You think Mathew McConaughey is gay? I asked.

I'm going to bed, she said to Aimee, looking at her as if she expected her to follow.

It's almost over, Aimee said, and she stayed with me on the couch. Our toes were touching, and we weren't wearing socks.

XI.

The other way I can go is exotic coffees and teas.
I can get them on discount because of the café.
They'll send a selection to Aimee each month, both cof-
fee and tea.

I like having new choices. You try one thing and like
it, but when a new cycle starts, something new arrives.

XII.

Claire is brushing her hair before the window. It's red and long and so pretty it makes me sad. The sun is coming in.

I can go either way, I tell her. Movies or coffee and tea?

Claire makes that face, the one that says, Get lost.

When she leaves the apartment, I see her walk to her Toyota in a short skirt.

The lowriders across the street stop working on their cars and watch her.

I watch them.

I like those white tank-top undershirts Chicano boys wear. I like how their cars hop up and down, the way they love their women, how a single arm pulls her by the neck to him, and he kisses her and then lets her go.

XIII.

Julio hates cholos.

They're pigs, he says.

Julio's a big queen.

You can see it watching him through the café windows from the street, the way he moves.

With me, people can't always tell. Aimee, when she was still new, asked me flat out, Are you gay?

We were both wiping off a table, getting it ready for some guy who was waiting right there, holding his books and a laptop. She looked at me for an answer, but I just finished wiping the table and went back behind the counter. I was the barista that day. When she came up and ordered some drinks, she asked, Well, are you?

I am, I said.

Cool, she said. Me too.

Pure gay or bi? I asked.

I gave up that *bi* shit a long time ago, she said, snapping the towel at me, like we were two boys in the shower.

XIV.

I chose chick flicks.

Aimee opens the gift, and when she sees what I got her, she jumps up and down. She comes in and hugs me.

When do you want to watch the first one? she asks.

Tonight, I say.

Not tonight, Claire says.

Claire is taking Aimee out for her birthday.

XV.

Aimee is getting ready in front of the bathroom mirror. I'm sitting on the closed toilet seat watching her. She stops putting stuff on her face and looks at me, like she's concerned. She tilts her head.

You really need to find yourself a guy, she says.

You think, I say?

Someone special, she says.

Someone special, I repeat.

Yeah! Any new prospects at work? she asks.

I would answer her, but the bells start their tune,

> *Dum dum da-dum dum.*
> *Dum dum da-dum dum.*

XVII.

I was a Christian once.

I went to a humongous church with thousands of other people. I had a girlfriend then. Her name was Heather Pinkerton. We went to services on Wednesdays and Sundays, and took Bible study on Tuesday evenings.

I remember one Sunday the pastor preached about how sometimes we don't know what to pray for, but we feel something in our gut. We can just groan, he said. The Holy Spirit knows what we need, he said. The Holy Spirit will convert our groans into prayers.

Now, as I'm sitting on the toilet seat watching Aimee get ready, the bells are groaning the hour.

Bong.

Bong.

Bong.

Sábado Gigante

At first, when the boys picked their teams, baseball teams, football teams, soccer teams, they assumed I would be a good player, because of my large size, and because of my name, Bruno, seriously, Bruno. My father was as large as a WWF wrestler, his muscles so bulging that the tattoos on his forearms seemed to pulse. He taught me to box when I was four years old, or tried to, but one time he left me with a bloody nose, and after that I refused to learn. Whenever he pulled out the boxing gloves and walked over to me, before he could even tie the first one on my wrist, I was bawling my eyes out, until my mom came over, wrapped me up in her arms and carried me away from him.

He told her that I was a disappointment, that maybe I should have been a girl that my name should be Hilda, which he started to call me for a time, but only around the house. He wanted my weakness to be a family secret, so he made sure I looked and talked tough in front of everyone else. They dressed me like a miniature version of him, in work boots and Ben Davis work pants, and I wore thick lumberjack flannels and buttoned them up to the neck. By the time I was in sixth grade, I was big as a gorilla. I had to look down on my teachers when they scolded me or tried to tell me I was smart and should take school subjects more seriously. Boys made assumptions about me, one of them that I was good at sports and they'd want me to play with them, but by the next game, when we chose new teams, I was the last one picked.

My neighbor Carlo, a short, muscular little guy, was one of the best players in the neighborhood, a boy's boy, and he was usually a team captain, and because he was my best friend, he picked me second or third every time, even though he knew he was wasting a turn. He wanted to believe in me, wanted to believe that somewhere inside of me there was a ball player trying to get out, but he was losing his faith. One day, on the way out to the field, he reached up and grabbed my shoulders from behind and massaged me like a trainer sending his fighter into the ring. "Sábado Gigante!" he said, his nickname for me. "Let's get them, Sábado," he said. Then he punched me on the arm, and although it burned like hell, I was happy to get it, because I knew it was the way he expressed affection.

He took the game very seriously that day, screaming to his team when they messed up, yelling things at the batter when he was pitching. When a fly ball came right to me, dropping from the clouds like a slow bomb, something anyone could catch, I held up my glove and closed my eyes hoping that it would land in the cradle of my hand, but when I heard the ball thump on the ground a few feet away from me, I opened my eyes. The first thing I saw was Carlo shaking his head, disappointed in me, mouthing curses at me.

After that inning, as we were walking up to the batters' cage, I pretended to fall. I pretended to twist my ankle.

"I should sit this one out," I told him.

He nodded his head, patted me on the shoulder.

I went inside the house. My mom was home, in the bedroom reading a book. I went into my room and played with my GI Joe figurines and little green plastic soldiers. I pretended that they were actors and I was a giant director, literally a giant making a blockbuster movie. I yelled *Action!* and moved the soldiers around to play out my 30-minute movie. After a soldier was shot and killed or torn to pieces in an explosion, I yelled, *Cut!* And the little man wiped himself off and stood up again.

Later on, when I knew the ballgame was over, I went back outside, saying what a bummer it was that I couldn't play. "We could have rolled some heads," I told Carlo.

He was taking off his T-shirt. "Right," he said as he draped it over his shoulder.

One day, when the boys were off paying ball, I stepped outside and saw Gracie Gómez playing dolls on a pink blanket in her front yard. She was Carlo's sister, and I looked at her sitting on her spread-out blanket moving a doll around as if it were taking a walk. It occurred to me that since Carlo and I were best friends, Gracie was almost like family. She was like my little sister, so I went over to her. I walked over to her lawn and said "Hey," and she said "Hey."

Ten minutes later I was playing dolls too.

From that day on, I never wanted to play sports again, ever, just dolls, because you made up characters with stories and dialogue. You could imagine the houses they had, the jobs they did, the cities in which they lived. Gracie liked playing dolls with me, because together we imagined so much more than mommy and daddy dialogues. We were international spies, or we were young doctors in the emergency room, or we were homicide detectives, looking over the murder scene, gathering clues. Our favorite dolls were Raggedy Ann and Andy, although we gave them different names for different lives, Mr. and Mrs. Martínez, Pepe and María. We also played with a bunch of other, smaller dolls, who became their family and friends, but Ann and Andy were always the stars of our little movies, which we imagined took place in places like Paris, London, Peru, Mexico City.

We had fun together, more fun than I ever had with Carlo, because being with him felt like work, but with her I could play, and for a time, a very short time, I was convinced that Gracie and I were best friends.

Her parents were from Puerto Rico, hard workers and traditional Catholics, and the only boys she was allowed to talk to were family members, including me, because our families had been neighbors for years. Unlike my mother, who worked full time and took classes at the community college, her mother stayed at home taking care of the kids and the house. Her father wanted to raise his daughter to be the same way, and she had three brothers, all of them like Carlo, boys who wanted to be men.

We both knew we had to hide the things we did together.

She never came to my door and asked for me. We came up with secret codes, and when I saw her pink blanket draped over the fence in our backyards, I knew she would be in the alley waiting for me with her dolls and accessories. Without saying anything, or else whispering, we'd tiptoe to the side of my house, where my father's 1953 Ford pickup truck had been sitting for years, all the tires flat, the windshield coated with dirt. Gracie set the pink blanket down on the bed, spreading out all her toys, and we got into the back of the truck and played.

One Saturday afternoon, Gracie and I were in the back of my father's truck playing dolls when I saw the boys coming around the corner down the alley. They had bats over their shoulders and baseball mitts dangling from their ends. Carlo had his T-shirt off, tied around his head like an Arab, and his skin was dark brown and sweaty. Walking in the lead, all the other boys walking behind him, he looked like a soldier returning from war. I could hear them laughing like boys, talking to each other, hitting metal garbage cans with their bats, chasing away alley cats. Gracie wrapped up her dolls and their things in her blanket, and she swooped it all away and ran to the tall fence that our backyards shared, pushed a loose board and went through, and on her lawn, she spread out the blanket and hoped to look like she had been playing by herself. I jumped out of the back of the truck, uncertain whether or not Carlo had seen us. From down the throat of the alley, he squinted his eyes to get a better look at me. The boys got closer, and Carlo went to the gate that opened onto his backyard, slammed it open, and saw her sitting on her blanket playing dolls by herself. I couldn't see her, only a blur of her colors through the slats of the fence, but he was yelling something to her in Spanish, and I saw her pink blur slide up and move across the yard toward the house, and I heard the door open and close and the blur disappeared inside.

"What were you doing with my sister?" Carlo asked me, walking toward me, all the boys behind him.

"What are you talking about?"

"Why was she in the truck with you?"

"What? No! She came over the house for some girl's thing. I think your mom wanted to tell my mom something. I don't know. So when are we going to play ball? Did I miss the game?"

"We're taking a break," said another boy. "You want to play next innings?"

"You bet!" I said. "Whose team am I on?"

They looked around at each other, but Carlo was still looking at me as if my face might reveal something.

"We were just talking," I said. "Can I play next innings? I need a glove. Someone lend me their glove."

The next day or so I saw Gracie playing with her dolls on a blanket on the front lawn, and seeing that no one was around, I went to join her. "Let's meet in the truck," I said.

She looked coldly at me and continued to play, imaging a dialogue between a mommy and a daddy. In an exaggerated deep voice, she said, "I'm going to work now, honey!"

"We're having spaghetti for dinner tonight," she said, in a feminine voice.

"Hey," I said.

She nodded a greeting but continued to play.

"I want to play," I said.

She started to gather her stuff in a pile. "It's not right," she said. She piled everything together, wrapped it in the blanket, twisted the top, and she walked away from me, dragging all the things behind her.

Exegesis

One morning, as he was sitting on his oversized arm-chair reading a novel, the too-loud doorbell pulled him away from the dream. He stood up, took the book with him to the living room, and when he opened the door, Preciosa Sánchez stood on the porch in a bright red business suit, holding a big black purse.

"It looks really good!" she said. She sounded so excited, her big brown eyes looking around the house and the yard. "Estoy bien surprised."

The reader half-expected to see cobblestone streets of the old city where the cats swirled around like dust devils, but it was the desert city in which he lived, and it was so windy that morning that he could barely see through the brown air to the foot of the mountain across the street from his house. Preciosa held her hands over her eyes to protect them from the sting of hot dust, and she yelled through the wind, "Now I see what you mean!"

A Mexican alder, not much taller than the house, slapped its branches against the wall as if manic to get in. He told Preciosa to come inside, and once he closed the door, the gust of hot wind that followed her in died out, and the remaining sand fell to the floor like glittery mites. She walked across the room, and the clothes on her body strained to keep her in. "This is a different place," she said. "When did you do all this?"

She walked past him to peek into the hallway, and he could smell her bath soap, clean, fresh like a schoolgirl. She walked down the hallway, so awed by what she saw that she put her hands over her mouth. He followed behind her and could see her figure reflected in the hardwood floors, could smell the trail of shampoo in her hair, thick, black, and still slightly wet. This was her first appointment of the day. She walked into the library, which had built-in bookshelves and plantation shutters and the leather armchair where he had been reading the novel.

"¡Dios mío! This is muy linda!"

He was going to put the novel down on the small table next to the chair, but there was something about its heaviness in his hands that he liked to feel, that he felt he needed to feel, as if the weight of an anchor, all that kept him from floating off the floor until his body pressed against the ceiling. He followed her through the house, into a circle of doors from room to room to room. When she stepped out to the backyard, she walked into his garden, around which he had built a stone wall, and she let out an excited gasp. The wisps of wind swirled around the top of the tall walls like notes of a cello, trying to enter the garden.

In the kitchen, they sat down and had coffee, under the cold air of the new air conditioner. "I think we can sell esta casa," she said. "I might tell my tía about this. Le gustaría, I'm sure. She lives in Juaritos, ¿la conoces? That's what we call Juárez. All those murders every day and bodies piled up in mass graves, it's not safe no more. Después de tantos años, she's agreed to come to El Paso. I could see her living here in this house."

The reader looked around the shine and wood of his house.

"Se llama Juana. My aunt? She never goes no where, de veras, pero está vieja and no puede cuidarse a sí misma, by herself. ¿Entiendes? She gets to where she talks to herself like she was talking to invisible people."

Something moved in the other room, and he looked through the doorway and saw the leather armchair by the window, the shadow of the Mexican alder moving in the wind.

"One time, she got up in the middle of the night and started making tamales! I mean, she had all the stuff out there and she starts making hundreds of tamales like there was going to be a wedding or a big party."

The reader held the book close to his chest. He wondered why the aunt had the ingredients in her house to make hundreds of tamales.

"No lo sé. Está loca. She started cooking at three in the morning. She worked all night long, boiling the pork, spreading the masa on the leaves, making the salsa, so that by morning time, the smell of tamales filled the barrio and people woke up smelling them. They smelled so good. ¡Ay! La vecina—her name is Meche—we call her la metiche—you know what that means, ¿qué no?—It's like someone who always butts in, well, Meche la metiche went over to find out what was going on, and my tía gave her a dozen tamales. Meche said they were the best she ever tasted in her whole entire life. But the weird thing is . . . "

Preciosa leaned across the table to get closer. She whispered, "The weird thing is that once the tamales were gone, Meche wanted more. She couldn't think of anything else but getting more. She said that each bite was like a fantasy. That's how she said it. A fantasy. That's weird, ¿qué no? Fantasy Tamales.

"And this woman está muy vieja y flaquita flaquita. I ask you, who could she have been making all those tamales for? Who? What fantasy world was she in?"

He was enjoying the story, and he wanted to picture the aunt as beautiful.

Was she a beautiful woman?

"My tía beautiful? ¡No, es muy fea! She looks like a frog. Why do you ask?

"Anyway, Meche went back to check on her, you know, and she tells us that my aunt was setting up tables, as if there would be a big party, and she was dressed all nice too, like it was Easters. Meche asked my aunt if her family was coming to visit her from El Paso, but my aunt just gave her another dozen tamales—like to shut her up, no? And then she sent a boy to the store for her, and he brought back a bunch of bottles of wine, a whole bunch, and she had everything ready for a big fiesta. But she forgot to invite the people! There were all these tables set up inside her house, una pachanga de verdad, but it was for people who didn't exist.

"Anyhow, we think she should live near la familia, you know? I think she would like it here in this house. Pero I don't know. Conflict of interest and all, pero, necesitamos hacer algo. Pobre mujer. El otro día la vecina—you know, Meche?—she saw my aunt walking around the streets with a cloth bag—it had the image of la virgin, she was collecting rocks. She examined them, rock by rock, looking for something in the core of each rock. Some she took, and others she left there on the street, right where she picked them up."

Preciosa took a drink of her coffee, made a face because it was cold by now, and she put down her cup but didn't let it go. She had chubby cheeks, and her perpetual dimples made it seem like she was still smiling.

"She would like it here, en esta casa, pero that might be conflict of interest, ¿verdad?"

She shrugged her shoulders.

"No, no," she said, looking inside her cup, as if reading the coming of sadness in the swirl of coffee grains.

Leeky's Birthday

The fear of a lion is how your brain chemically translates your body's desire to stay home, to *not* take a shower, to not get dressed and get into the car and drive through hot, inner city traffic.

The sluggard says, 'There's a lion outside! I'll be killed in the public square!'"

You don't want to go to your nephew's fifth birthday party, since it means you'll have to buy him a gift, and you're approaching broke, because the check you wrote for last month's rent still hasn't gone through. It means you have to get ready and drive across town to see him. It means all the family will be there, your other brothers, your sisters, all of their spouses and kids, and your father snapping pictures of everyone *ad naseum* with his Leica 50 mm.

You don't want to admit to yourself that you don't love your brother enough to go, and you really think you do love him enough to go, because sometimes when you think of him—like that day you got caught in the rain and you thought you saw him in a café window sitting at a table by himself—you feel a quick jerk in your heart, something pleasant, and you have always translated that feeling as love.

So you have to justify staying home. You know your brother really wants you to go—he begged you on the phone, *Please come, it'll mean a lot to Leeky, I'm serious, bro, please come*—so your brain must create an image that justifies your desire to stay home.

Enter the lion.

In French: *Il y a un chacal qui barre la route, un lion parcourt les rues!*

There is a lion in the streets and the public places, in the mall, the parks, in the Walmart where you would have bought your nephew a gift. It is the city's rise in crime, and you don't want to be another victim. It's your fear of standing in line at the checkout for hours, pressed so close to the unkillable poor. It is the poor, old men breathing in your face, kids touching everything with toxic hands, old women coughing their spittle into your breathable air. You hate putting up with those people, who unfortunately remind you of your brother and his family, the young dad with Chicano tattoos, a young mother with long black hair like a Mexican dancer, the three kids screaming and whining, the youngest, Leeky, his nose crusted with snot, and the oldest, 14 years old, a boy on the brink of being a banger.

You don't want to leave your house for your brother's house, for Leeky's birthday party, because you don't want to work that hard. You want only to stay home with all the curtains drawn and the TV on, so you create lions.

But there's something else.

In the first clause of the French translation, it doesn't say lion, but *chacal*, jackal, which in Hebrew reads, "Said a lazy man Jackal in the way; Lion amid the plaza."

There are lions and jackals waiting to pounce on you, so you better stay home.

Maybe it's your ex-wife, whom you fear you might see in the public places, whom you fear today might be out there also buying your brother's kid a gift.

You know she was invited to Leeky's birthday party by your brother's wife, Jazmín. Those two women are very close, like sisters, and Jazmín has a sister too, Carmen, and together they are like three sisters. At parties they always stand together, in a semi-circle, laughing at something the other had said or thought (it was like they knew what the others were thinking), or they whispered stories to each other, holding each other's hands. You are afraid of them, of their spiritual power, because when they are together, they are strong.

One time, when you were still married to your ex, you walked in on them. They were in the kitchen, red curtains, black refrigerator, and they were in a circle talking. You just wanted to pour yourself another whiskey and Coke, and the ice was in the freezer. When they noticed your presence, they all turned their necks at the same time and looked at you.

"I'm sorry," you said, and you held up your empty glass. "I just wanted more ice." You stood there, and your brother's wife, Jazmín, was wearing a long black and red skirt, with a white stone medallion around her neck. She looked like a pagan priestess. She gave you a mean look, as if you were intruding, and they all looked at you like that, even your wife. You thought that you forgot how to breathe, and you tried to catch your breath.

Finally your wife said, "Well, get your ice then."

Mujeres Matadas

"Hey, viejo. Ready for some rock and roll?" said the girl. She was standing right next to me at the bar, paying for her beer, but she was so small I had to look down.

"Rock and roll!?" I said. "I thought this was a Neil Diamond tribute!"

She smiled and said, "Have fun" as she walked back to the stage, back to her guitar. She was Mexican, probably from Juárez. Her accent was strong.

Her amp was plugged in, and she was testing her guitar with some rock riffs, "Iron Man" by Black Sabbath, "Wish You Were Here" by Pink Floyd.

The fat drummer was warming up too, pounding out some beats, and in spite of his large mass, he was fast, his arms blurring as he pounded those drums. Two skinny boys were on guitar and bass, and that was the band; two guitars, a bass and a drum set.

The way I liked it. That was all you needed to play rock and roll, any rock and roll, death metal, heavy metal, black, gothic, whatever kind of rock, just four instruments and vocals. One of the skinny boys set his guitar on a stand and grabbed the microphone and said, "One, two, three."

The girl came in on the guitar, a death metal beat, *fffoo fffoo fffoo fffoo,* and then the drums came in and the bass, and it was loud, and it was good, and the boy clasping the microphone started singing into the cup of his hands, and like a lot of death metal voices, his was raspy and loud, indistinguishable from other voices of death, just another instrument like the guitar, loud, distorted. Who could tell what he was saying? Together the guitar and the voice were like roars, and it got to me.

I liked it.

Kids started running into the mosh pit, and they ran around in circles, young, plump and skinny kids, running in both directions.

And when I say kids, I mean, in their twenties. Kids to me.

They ran so fast, around and around, as if frenzied by the music, and as they passed each other in opposite directions, they brushed against each other, almost slamming into each other, but not quite. It wasn't violent like other mosh pits I had witnessed (and participated in), but cute, like children playing in a field. And this was El Paso in 2010, so almost all the kids in the club were Mexican, Latino, Chicano, whatever term it was they used to indicate themselves. I had lived the last thirty years in LA, where Mexicans were everywhere, but here it was different, if only because white people on this border city were more than the minority, they were rare. There were a lot of light-skinned people in El Paso, blondes with blue eyes and freckles on their cheeks, but they were more likely to speak Spanish than English, and even if some of them may have felt themselves superior to indios, they were still Mexicans.

I walked closer to the stage, because I wanted to get a closer look at the band. The girl was "in the zone," as they say, her eyes closed as her flingers slid up and down the width of the neck, playing *one, two, three—one, two, three* and then subverting it with a hard *one* and a hard *one* and a hard *one, two, three* again.

The boy on vocals put the mike on the stand and picked up his guitar. He took over the rhythm that the girl was playing, and she started on lead. Her fingers fluttered fast, like locusts over rows of wheat fields, and people yelled and whistled. I couldn't help it. I whistled. She was that good.

I must have been standing there for a while, my body moving to the music while my mind wandered into a labyrinth of memories and thought, and suddenly the music was over.

The boy told everyone their CDs were for sale, and then the bar manager came on stage and said the next band would be called "Dead Gabriel."

I went to the bar to order another drink. On stage, the girl was rolling up her cord. The fat drummer was carrying his stuff off stage, like a little boy taking his toys home. I gulped down my whiskey and ordered another one and gulped that down too.

Finally I was feeling a little happy drunk, energetic drunk. I wanted to hear more music, more intensity. I didn't want to let my mind enter my mother's house, the dark windows, the dusty floors or the wooden shack in the back, where the only light came from when the doors were pulled open and the sun shot in and shone on the piles of junk, stuff my mother hoarded over fifty years. A bike from my youth covered in dust and cobwebs hung on the wall. My mother was a hoarder, and I wondered how long I would have to stay in El Paso before I was able to get rid of all the stuff, sell the house and go back home to my wife and dogs?

"So what did you think, old man?" She was standing there at the bar. I could barely hear her because of the music they played between bands, loud death metal en español.

Machete en mano

Y sangre india

"Sounded like a bunch of noise to me," I said.

She laughed and pointed at me and squinted her eyes. "You're a liar. You liked it very much, I think."

"Seriously. You play well," I said. "You were great."

The boy brought her a beer. She took a drink.

She looked at me, then walked over to me. She had dark green eyes.

"Can I sit here?" she asked about the bar stool next to me.

"Yeah, of course," I said. I even backed up my stool to give her a bit more room.

She climbed up the stool and straddled it like it was a horse. Her cheeks were thin, sunken in, like you could imagine the shape of her skull. She took a drink of beer. Looked at the label, interested in everything. She had long fingers with rings on almost all of them. "You like this kind of music?" she asked, indicating the song on the speakers.

I recognized the band, a death metal group from Mexico.

"Brujería's all right." I said.

She raised her eyebrows, as if she were impressed with my knowledge.

"Do you know what they're singing?" she asked.

"Matanda güeros."

"¡Qué chulo!" she said, surprised. "You know the music even!"

"Not bad for an old, man, huh? What's your name?" I asked.

She took a cocktail napkin, wrote something on it and slid it over to me. It said *Mari(a)*.

"How do you pronounce it?" I asked.

She shrugged her shoulders. "You tell me, viejo."

She looked at me as if she wanted to tell me something but was unsure, but then she said it, leaning in a bit.

"Look, I just want you to know that I'm just being friendly, okay? I wouldn't get the wrong idea, you know? I'm not into old men."

I nodded, held up my left hand, showing her my gold band.

She took a drink of her beer, looked at me and said, "You remind me of my uncle. That's all."

"Who's your uncle?"

"He's dead."

"Sorry."

"Juárez," she said, as if that explained it all.

The drummer came by and stood in front of Mari(a)'s stool. She introduced him as Beto. Then a few of their friends came by, and now a bunch of them were chattering and laughing, me in the middle of them like a chaperone.

She said, "Hey, guys. This is my uncle. He came to see me play."

Everyone referred to her as Mari and to me as "sir."

Beto asked me what I thought of the music.

"Prefiero rancheras," I said. "Vicente, música así."

Mari(a) was the only one who laughed at my joke, and she punched me on the arm, and with all her rings it kind of hurt.

Dead Gabriel was the best band of the night. From Austin, the lead singer was a black kid with so much energy he ran around the stage in short bursts, his voice pure rage. He had a 1970s style afro, like Billy Preston, the round of it blurring as he moved his head. His voice vibrated on the walls, the floors, on my arms, and in their best song of the night, I realized what made him so good was that it was *his* voice, death metal style, but with clarity and precision.

> *Let the dead*
> *Bury their dead!*
> *Let the dead*
> *Bury their dead!*

As if pulled by their force, Mari(a) and some of the kids and I got up off our stools and walked closer to the stage, so we could look up at them, sway with them, raise our fists with them. We even started to jump up and down. Every now and then Mari(a) and I looked at each other and mouthed, "Fuck!"

> *Jesus said*
> *Fuck the dead*
> *Let the dead . . .*

And then they were done.

We stood there.

"Wow," she said. "They were good."

We walked back to the bar and I bought us both another drink.

"So why do you like death so much?" she asked. "We don't see too many . . . "

"Old people? How old do you think I am?"

"Fifty," she said.

"On the nose," I said. "And you, María?"

"Twenty-two," she said. "So what do you like about death?"

I thought about it, looking for a canned response in the shelves of my memory, but I remembered that I had never been able to find an answer. One time my wife walked in on me when I was working on my computer in my office at home, the death metal blasted so loud I didn't hear her come in. I thought she was at work, and when I looked up and saw her standing in the doorway, the sunlight shooting in, she looked down on me as if she had caught me masturbating. I turned down the music.

"Is everything all right?" I asked, standing up.

"Why do you like that crap?" she asked.

I wasn't able to answer her. I said, "I just like it."

"But why?" asked Mari(a). "Why do you like it?"

"It's evil," I said.

"That's why you like it?"

"I mean, I'm not into Satan or anything like that." I took a drink of my whiskey. "Sometimes you need to feel it."

"So, do you want to see something really evil?"

"What do you mean?" I asked, looking at her as if horns were about to sprout from her head.

"Do you like Black?"

"Black metal? Like Gongoroth?"

"Darker. Real evil. I could show you some bands."

I laughed, wondering what she thought would be evil. I had been in town for a few weeks, and I had seen almost every metal show that I could. What could she show me? And as I watched her face look at me as if she held a secret, I remembered how young she was, how much she hadn't yet experienced.

I looked around the club at all the kids. "They try to be dark around here," I said. "In the mosh pit they run around in circles high-fiving each other as they pass, like kids playing 'Ring Around the Rosies.' No one ever gets hurt."

"Is that what you want to see?"

"No, that's not the point. It's just such a friendly release of energy, like a mosh pit in heaven. In California, I've seen mosh pits where . . . People let go. Their rage."

"Well, anyway, I'm not talking about El Paso." She straightened up. "I'm talking about Juárez. There's some underground clubs."

"Juárez? I thought the clubs were dying over there. That's what I read. Many of the businesses are moving to El Paso, you know. Restaurants. Nightclubs. There all moving here."

"I said underground."

"In Juárez?" I wasn't sure if I believed her.

"I'm talking hardcore Black, tío. Negro Metal. Maybe you would not be able to handle it," she said, her accent so strong she sounded like a foreign actress, like Penelope Cruz, even though she wasn't a Spaniard, but a middle-class Mexican. "It will not be so comfortable as here."

"I don't know. I've seen some pretty evil things in my life. Maybe some of them *you* would not be able to handle."

"Okay, tell me," she said.

"I used to live in Mexico City."

"So please tell me your dark adventures in el DF."

An image popped into my head, a murdered woman in an alley, behind some garbage cans, stray dogs sniffing around her body, but then I remembered that the image wasn't something I had seen in real life, but in a book I had read when I lived for a year in Mexico City.

"Do you want to go or not? I'll take you there."

"Isn't Juárez a bit dangerous right now?" I asked.

"What isn't dangerous?" she said. She took a drink from her beer bottle. "All these guys in the band I play with. They won't go. They're too scared."

"But you're not?"

"It's my home. I will never be afraid to go home. The place I'm talking about is like a guerrilla movement. They set up in some abandoned building. They play, and then they move on."

"You're making this up," I said.

"Trust me. And it's safe. You can take me. I don't have a car."

"You want me to drive in Juárez?"

"There's one on Friday. Wanna go?"

"I don't want to drive," I said.

"Don't be such a gringo. You'll be fine."

"Even the US government warns citizens not to go to Mexico, especially Juárez. It's the murder capital of the world."

"Oh, so you're very sure that you do whatever the US government tells you to do?"

"No, that's not it."

"Do you want to go or not?"

"I don't want to drive. I got California plates. I'll get carjacked."

"You know who's playing at this event? Las Mujeres Matadas."

"The murdered women?"

"They're an all-girl, black-metal group."

"That's . . . that's unusual."

"They'll give you nightmares."

I took a sip of whiskey, and I was drunk by now, and had it been Friday, I would have said, Sure, let's go. Instead I said, "I'll think about it."

"You can pick me up at eight p.m."

"Where do you live?"

"By UTEP."

"Are you a student?"

She nodded, and suddenly I felt that all this was innocent after all, that she was bluffing, that if anything, I reminded her of her uncle and that reminded her of Juárez, her amor por Juárez, and she just wanted to imagine going into the city, going back home. She was just a bourgeois kid.

"Gee, I haven't asked this in a long time," I said. "What's your major?"

"Philosophy," she said.

"Figures," I said.

She handed me a piece of paper with handwriting on it, and at first glance, I didn't recognize an order to the letters and numbers, not even the symbols, as if it were written in some ancient language, some secret code—and my heart skipped a beat. But then my eyes adjusted, and I saw that it was her address written on a cocktail napkin, "2199 Prospect. #3. 79902."

And a little note that said, "8 P.M."

When Mari and I drove into Juárez on Friday evening, there was still sun enough to see what the drug wars had done. It looked pretty much the same to me, pharmacies and liquor stores and restaurants, the only difference being the army trucks full of young Indian soldiers carrying automatic rifles. They were patrolling the streets, parked on busy intersections, short Indian boys holding rifles, boys too young for facial hair.

It wasn't until we entered deeper into the city, away from the border, that I saw how different the city had become during wartime. On intersection light poles, on the sides of buildings, on stone fences, there were posters and fliers with the pictures of young girls, posted by their families, ladies who were doing all they could to get their girls back, Lupita Pérez Montes, Esmeralda Monreal, Nancy Muñoz, *Ayúdanos a buscarlas.*

I was afraid to be in Juárez in my car in the impending night, but somehow having Mari(a) next to me in the passenger's seat made me feel safer, maybe because she wasn't afraid.

Many of the businesses were boarded up, weeds growing out of the cement in the parking lots, and many buildings had been demolished and stood in piles of rubble like bombs had gone off.

"Fucking sad, you know?" she said, looking at piles of rubble on a corner, a building that used to be a mini mall. "I used to fucking shop there, man," she said, shaking her head as if she couldn't believe it. We drove onto a narrow street lined with dentist offices and tailor shops and discount stores, then a few larger stores full of people going in and out. We passed by a storefront with big display windows onto the street, and inside, behind a barrier of sandbags, was a soldier, pointing his rifle at the street, at us.

We passed the Hotel Juárez, a corner building with a façade of turquoise-colored tile, like it might have been pretty fancy a long time before. Maybe when I was a teenager, sneaking in and out of Juárez with my friends, that hotel was luxurious, maybe it had a ballroom with gilded walls and a chandelier.

But then there were parts of the city that seemed so normal: a park with a bunch of people hanging out, teenagers melting into each other's bodies, kids playing in the open air, vendors pushing carts of paletas and snow cones, just like any other city.

"You know what really fucking pisses me off?" she asked. "Turn here."

I turned where she asked me to, and we drove down an abandoned road with nothing on the side but dry land and rock. A housing development appeared up ahead, one of those suburban tracks with an entrance and a sign, like Agrestic in *Weeds*. It was a new development, the houses modern with two stories and the garages pushed up front. Each house had a small yard and big double doors.

But the homes were empty. If they weren't boarded up, they were abandoned, the windows busted out, doors knocked in. Some of the houses had debris all over the front yard. Some of them had spray paint across the garage doors, *¡Sálvanos!* and other more profane expressions.

"Stop," she said, and I braked in front of a house that wasn't boarded up but that had signage all over warning about keeping away. Signs were everywhere: spray-painted on the walls, posted on stakes in the yard, written on the door. *Keep out! Go away!*

It hadn't worked. The place looked pillaged.

"That's my house," she said. "Or was."

"What happened?" I asked.

Over thirty years ago, when I was in high school, I used to cross into Juárez at night, a bunch of us kids ready to party and lose our minds, and we were so skinny and light with youth that we floated across the bridge like naughty angels and stumbled back like the happy dead. We did dollar-tequila shots and drank bottles of beer, and sometimes we paid ten bucks to get into a club that had a deejay and a barra libre, and we drank so much beer and sweet, blended drinks that our bellies burst and we barfed just to make more room.

Drunk and together with our crazy friends, a bunch of us would skip our way down Avenida Juárez to a taco place and stuff our mouths and tummies with greasy meat and cheese wrapped in a stack of corn tortillas as we drank cans of cold Tecate. Street kids came to our table begging for money and food, and we bought them bottles of Fanta and gave them quarters. We were only teenagers, years away from the legal right to drink on the other side of the bridge, but in Juárez, we felt like adults.

The city was our playground, a nighttime labyrinth of possibilities, and because we were full of hormones, we used our freedom to make-out in public, feel each other up at the clubs, at dark tables or in underground hall-ways that led to the bathrooms. Some of us had sex in the bathroom stalls, and when it was over, we did lines on the backs of the toilets.

This was when Juárez was safe, or so we believed.

Turns out that it was never safe.

But we were safe, or we felt like it.

Even when we passed by Juárez police on our drunken-boat walk back to the bridge, back to our side of the border, as the cops looked at us, sometimes shaking their heads at us, we continued to laugh and talk loudly, sometimes yelling so loud at each other it was like we wanted everyone to hear us, wanting others to witness our youth.

Some of the girls with us walked back in short skirts and high heels, and the men standing idle on the corners watched them as they bent over to take off their shoes, carrying them by the straps, walking barefoot across the concrete screaming, *Woo!!!*

But that was then, when Juárez seemed safe.

Or safer.

There were always stories our parents told us in order to warn us about the dangers of getting drunk in

Juárez, which is how the fact of the murdered women first came to our attention. There were stories, rumors, about a girl missing, a girl walking home from the factory, a girl from Michoacán, from Sinaloa, Veracruz, Quintana Roo, and then there were sporadic articles in the *El Paso Times*, the bodies of girls on the sides of barren hills, dead girls found only because their young hands were spotted sticking out of garbage heaps, as if trying to grab on to something, or an ankle would be coming out of a mound of dirt and rock, girls barely approaching puberty, their bodies mutilated, all of the parts being uncovered little by little, until we saw the whole horror of it, the numbers adding up, the murdered women, the murdered girls, the authorities pretending there was no problem or like they were doing something about a small problem at most.

And now there were the drug wars. Now Juárez had the dubious distinction of being the Murder Capital of the World, and women and girls were still disappearing, a lot of them, 16-, 17-year-old girls.

Since the drug wars, whenever I came back to El Paso to see my mother for some matter of her estate or health care, I avoided Juárez. Driving on Friday night with Mari(a) was my first time here since I was thirty years old. I remember I was right out of law school, my first year working with a firm in LA, the job I always dreamed of having. I was staying for a few days with my mom and my dad, who was still alive then, and I was helping him with some paper work, the company he worked at for forty years trying to deny his retirement. I filed papers. I studied documents. One night I walked across the Santa Fe Bridge and into downtown Juárez. I drank some beers at the Kentucky Club, which was full that night with a mixture of Juarenses and El Paso people. After a few beers, I wandered through Boys' Town, where I slipped into a place called Pigalle. I sat at a table by myself and watched the women at other tables surrounded by men and bottles of beer, the ladies laughing and controlling the hands of all the men groping them, like octopus women. I wasn't married then, and I must have been looking for something, because when a plump Indian-looking girl walked in, with big lips and wearing a ridiculously small outfit, I stared at her. She knew I was looking at her, and she looked at me, smiled and winked. I rose from my table.

Juárez.

Now I was driving around with a girl I had just met, and I went wherever she told me to go, and as it got dark, I got a little afraid. We found ourselves driving down a two-lane road out of the city. Nothing lined the road. We could see some lights in the distance, buildings somewhere far off, and in the distance, sirens wailed. We could see the El Paso star burning on the black mountain, but all else was dark, and we could only see what the headlights lit up in front of us, the white lines coming at us.

Mari said, "Here, you want this?"

She held two red pills in the palm of her hand.

"What is it?" I asked.

"What do you think?"

She told me to pull up to a cluster of buildings, which looked abandoned, surrounded by a chain-link fence. The gate to the parking lot had been torn off and was lying flat.

"Here?" I asked. "This is it? You said there'd be a concert."

The buildings reminded me of one those old insane asylums in the country, where they used to give electric shock treatments.

I took the pills from her palm, but she said, "Only one. The other one's for me."

I threw it in my mouth and swallowed, and she handed me a bottle of water.

"Give it about 20 minutes," she said. "Come on."

When we drove onto the side of the building, we saw there were a bunch of cars parked there.

"I told you. These shows are like a guerrilla movement. They set up in some abandoned building. They play, and then they move on."

We got out of the car and heard pounding coming from inside the building, which used to be a factory. The double metal doors were closed shut, and on them was written *¡Peligro! No ingresar,* and I could feel the bass pulsing from the other side, as if it might blow the doors off.

There was a man at the door in a dark suit and tie that looked like a secret service agent. He even had a wire in his ear. When he saw us coming, he stood before the door, and when we got there, Mari opened her palm and held a red poker chip. The security man nodded, and he turned to open the doors.

He grabbed both door handles with his big fists, and he pulled hard with a single jerk.

We watched the doors fly open like the wings of an angel, revealing a nighttime sky scattered with stars, and there was a moon as big as the sun.

The force of the music seemed to lift us to the middle of the floor, surrounded by hundreds of young people, boys with long hair, girls with black make-up. The stage was empty, except for some people setting up for the next band. People were standing around, drinking, yelling into each other's ears. The music was blasting from the speakers, and a few boys were in the mosh pit, forcefully banging against each other.

The song playing sounded like industrial noise, a repetitive whip.

Frrrrom.

Frrrrom.

"This place used to be one of the biggest maquiladoras in Juárez," Mari yelled into my ear. "A lot of the murdered women worked here in this very spot."

"It's huge," I said, looking around. It seemed the size of an indoor skating rink, high ceilings, with metal beams running across it. In the middle of the floor, separating the room, there was a counter, where maybe there used to be machinery for an assembly line. Now the Juárez kids were standing on it, drinking, moving to the beat.

"This is the last place some of the girls saw before they were murdered," she said.

Frrrrom.

Frrrrom.

"And the company bus," she continued, "picked them up right outside, but they dropped them off downtown. And they walked home alone."

I looked up and saw that part of the ceiling was falling in a giant chunk, and outside the moon was falling from space onto the floor, and I covered my head as if that would protect me from the debris all over my shoulders.

"It's kicking in, isn't it?" she asked.

"Maybe."

"I'll be right back," she said.

"Where are you going?" I said, not wanting to be left alone, but she vanished into the blur of bodies, and I had what must have been a vision: Lights came up and the music stopped and I saw the factory in full production, the whack of the machines, the buzzing of the saws, the women standing on the assembly line. Two European men in suits stood in an open door and watched one of the girls who worked walking into the bathroom.

Frrrrom.

The music stopped and the voices rose around me like dark vines.

I don't remember how long I walked around that dead factory, in and out of the past and present. I don't know how many groups played that night. I remember lights, I remember the moon shattering on the floor and I remember a mosh pit where shirtless young men rushed into each other, a fist, a head butt, and I remember that they carried more than a few boys out on stretchers, and I remember the announcer walking on stage, the lights blasting from behind him, and he introduced the next group, Juárez natives, "Las mujeres matadas."

The crowd exploded when they walked on stage, five young women, some of them wearing outfits like factory girls, dirty smocks, white lab coats spattered with blood, and a few of them wore Catholic schoolgirl skirts that were ripped and soiled and bloody. All their faces had make-up, as if they were zombies, white face, blood dripping from the eyes, and then they started their music and it was so hard and fast that I jumped up and down on my feet, and I'm not even sure at what point it occurred to me that the guitar player was Mari. She was wearing the Catholic schoolgirl skirt, but she didn't look sexy, didn't try to, she looked dead, murdered, angry as hell.

She had on skeleton make-up, a cross between black-metal style and the calaveras of the Day of the Dead, and she had a Frida Kahlo style scarf on her head.

Odio por Juárez
pa' esos hombres
es odio por Juárez.

Mari stepped forward and played lead, those fingers running back and forth like the legs of tiny people, the notes so fast and intense it felt like fleeing from the light of a nightmare you can't remember, the crowd growing in frenzy the quicker her fingers moved and all the other girls were watching as her guitar screamed pain and anger and it opened something in me and I walked in.

I don't remember what I did in there, but the landscape was pulsing with rage. I saw faces, bodies piled, lights glaring, shovels and picks, rocks and dirt and a kid's bicycle covered in sand. I saw my mother's body shriveled up under the covers, her eyes closed.

The band kept playing. I don't know what really happened or if it was the drug or if it's my memory now that I try and recall that night in Juárez, my perceptions of reality filtered by ego and past experience. I don't remember what I did while the Mujeres Matadas screamed for justice, for love of Juárez, I only know that I must've been inside that place for a while. And I remembered another song they played.

It was a black metal version of a Talking Heads song, "Life During Wartime."

This ain't no party
This ain't no disco
And I ain't fucking around.

Then they were done with it.

Mari became Mari again. She was out of breath, her chest moving up and down, but she was happy, not laughing and smiling, but fulfilled, as if the clouds broke open and the sun blasted her in warmth. She held her guitar like a rifle, and then she looked above the silhouette of heads that was the crowd, the lights shining in her eyes. She didn't look for me, didn't want to know what I thought of her performance. It wasn't about me. I had just met her the night before, and she asked me to take her to this concert, and I realized I was probably just a ride, a way to get here from the other side, someone she felt safe with. In fact, after it was all over and the lights came on and people left, I would look for her but wouldn't find her. The security men in dark suits would tell me to leave, and I would drive back to the border alone that night, figuring she must have left with some of her friends. But for now she was on stage shrouded in sweat and applause. She turned around and looked at the other Mujeres Matadas, all of them sweaty and done with it, too, all of them carrying instruments like weapons after the battle.

As the crowd whistled and yelled for them to play another song, as the motion around them blurred into a dull-colored background, the women looked at each other, the light in their eyes holding them together like a star.

Part IV

The The

The Michael Carver

. . . the aphasia of that heroic agony
of recalling a once loved number leading
slip by slipper to a general amnesia of misnomering . . .
Lucky in Godot

Charlotte and Sarah appeared around the rubble of the icehouse, walking into the field, both of them wearing clothes like we didn't normally see around town. Charlotte, tall with yellow hair, wore hip-hugger jeans and a blouse made of silky stuff that looked like a nightgown with thin straps.

Look at that! said Todd, like a perv, running his tongue across his teeth.

They're going to smoke out, said Danny.

Why else would anyone come into the field? It was dirt and rock and scattered with gutted washing machines and old tires, and the only two trees in the field, opposite each other—separated by a crumbling brick building, what used to be the icehouse—were leafless, shriveled-up old things. The boys were standing underneath one of them as if it still had shade, a crazy criss-crossing of branches cast on the dirt.

That Charlotte girl (the tall yellow-haired one) walked into the field like a queen, 100 percent sure the boys were watching her, and Sarah, a short Filipina girl, followed her like she was used to following her.

Damn! said Todd. *See that?*

Todd was tall and red-haired and freckled and he was thirteen years older than Danny and nine years older than me.

Danny shook his head, because he thought that Sarah (course he didn't know yet she was called Sarah) was the cuter of the two, because there was something about her, he thought, sumpin' different, maybe those Asian eyes.

Look, she's Filipina, he said to Todd.

She was short and chubby, and she wore a denim skirt and white tennis shoes.

I like Filipinas, said Danny, remembering the family that lived across the street from us until their mother got a better job and they left town.

Todd looked at Danny real hard. *You're stupid,* he said. *You can't tell the difference tween a Chinese girl and all those other kinds of Oriental girls . . . and pass me the bottle, butthead, you've been sucking on it for too long.*

She's Filipina, stupid, Danny said, and he was right on both counts. She was Filipina and Todd was stupid. *Look at her, anyone could tell.*

So Todd took the bottle from Danny and said, *There's all kinds of Oriental girls, not just Filipina.*

The two girls stopped underneath the only other tree, on the other side of the field, and in the cage of shade there was the backseat of a car, pulled from some old sedan, and Sarah sat there and Charlotte stood standing. Then, sure enough, Charlotte lit a spliff.

The boys wondered where they came from, and why they were in town. Not like there was a major highway through here, so they must have known someone who lived here, unless they were taking some road trip to nowhere and ended up in a town everyone in the world forgot about or never knew about, where every year the population got smaller and smaller and that City Limit sign—population 9,526—was just a joke. The old families had long spun out of there leaving only street names named after them and City Hall plaques about them that no one ever read anymore except one time Danny saw a plaque on the school wall that said The Michael Carver Memorial Gymnasium, and that was what everyone called it, The Michael Carver, like, "Meet you at The Michael Carver," and Danny thought it was weird to put "the" in front of a name, as if he were "The Danny Falcón" and Todd Bender was "The Todd Bender." I would have been The Rachel.

And Danny wondered who was the Michael Carver they had named the gym after, and when he asked the teachers, none of them knew and it bothered him that the building was named after someone nobody remembered, and one time, during P.E. he had forgotten something in his pants pocket, and he had to go back into the gym to get it, and it felt spooky walking down the empty cement halls of the boy's locker room, as if the ghost of Michael Carver was watching.

Across the street from the field was the old train depot, at the end of Oak Street, abandoned now, and Todd was staring at it as if he had seen a ghost. On the other side of the depot was what used to be a park (Hamilton Park it was called years back) that hadn't been cleaned since I was a kid, since the time the city council—when there still was a city council—sent a gang of cholos and bald white boys with tattoos on their necks out there in orange jumpsuits and green garbage bags to pick up bottles and papers and needles and diapers and to pull weeds.

I remember watching them from the window of our house, which was behind the park, all them cholos and poor white boys in orange suits, uncovering from a tangle of weeds the skeleton of what used to be a jungle gym, like they were pulling skin off a dead elephant.

Charlotte was walking around the car seat with a bunch of pent-up energy, like she had to do something, anything, had to keep moving, but Todd wasn't looking at her, he was looking at the train depot. He had a memory, one that came from his father, who one day said to him, he said, Todd, when I was a boy, *my* father (your grandpa) told me that the train depot that's still standing there today was where the GIs in Word War II went off to war. My father told me how he would go out there and watch the GIs kissing their girls goodbye, young women bending their knees behind them, and he saw their stockings and high-heeled shoes. Can you see it, Todd? The men looking like Kirk Douglas and Burt Lancaster, and all the women looking like Lauren Bacall.

When the whistles blew and the sergeants yelled, the GIs jumped on the train that pulled them away—some of them to never come back—and the handsome boys waved out the windows at the pretty young girls, waving and jumping until you couldn't see the train no more. Your granddad felt like crying just to see it.

Judging by Todd's eyes right now, it looked he might cry too, even though the memory had belonged to his father, long dead now, killed by a truck walking home one night on the highway. The train depot was abandoned now, a brick building with broken-out windows and tall grass growing all around, and even though trains still passed through town, they didn't stop. Todd looked at it sadly, like it was such a shame that we have to live in a world where we can't see girls named Betty and

Martha saying goodbye to slim young soldiers named Anderson and Blake.

Who could they be, those girls? Danny said, looking across the field. He was 12 years old now, and it was weird for me to see him with such long hair, hanging down straight and black, like a hippie kid, and he always had to pull it back to get it out of eyes so he could see.

Todd looked over there too, and he said, *I get the white girl. You can have the little brown one.*

He pictured himself kissing the yellow-haired girl (He didn't know her name would be Charlotte) and in his fantasy he saw himself movie-star handsome, dressed up like a GI coming home from war, and Charlotte dressed like a girl from back in the days of the war in a new dress with stockings and wearing a red hat.

Todd was 25. He shouldn't have been hanging around with Danny, because Danny was just a kid, and he definitely shouldn't have been checking out a girl Charlotte's age, 15, not even legal. Todd should have left right then, went home, but his mom was home, so he didn't even think about doing it, and even if he had thought of it, he would say, Naw! What am I gunna do at home but watch Alyssa Milano movies and masturbate?

Which one you like? Danny asked. *Cuz I like the Filipina.*

I told you, there's not just Filipino girls. There's Vietnamese girls and Japanese girls, did you ever think about that? Ever think she could be Japanese?

Todd noticed Charlotte stretch her body like she was waking from a nap—her yellow hair all catching the sun all beautiful girl-like—and she knew he was watching.

Charlotte yelled, *Hey, you guys wanna smoke out?*

Todd answered, *Hell yeah!* and walked over there.

But Danny didn't. He was too shy. He stayed put under that dying tree all by himself. He wondered what it would be like to—he didn't even have to kiss her—just to see the Filipina sitting on a couch, watching TV with him, with a bowl of popcorn on her lap.

I wanted to get him over there, because they needed to meet, not like she was the perfect girl for him and they were going to end up getting married or anything like that—I just saw what they would be like together.

A dog started barking at them from behind Danny, a dog behind the chain-link fence around some house.

Sarah stood up from the car seat and said, *What's wrong with him?*

He's stupid and shy, Todd said. *I'd just forget about him.*

She kept looking over there, maybe at the barking dog, or maybe because she thought it looked funny the way his mop of hair had a weird film of loose strands that were filled with light, or maybe what she noticed were the branches vibrating above him and making the twig shadow slant across his face like war paint. She laughed, because he was so small-townish and skinny but kind of cute, and you know you want to talk to him, so just go over there and do it.

Charlotte, hitting the joint, said to Todd, *You know where we can get some harder stuff?*

What kind of stuff you want? Todd asked.

What kind of stuff can you get?

Well there's H and meth and crack and up there in that house that used to be yellow is a guy named Hernández.

It was one of the few houses on that side of the field that still had someone living in it, Hernández, who had knocked down all the interior walls so he could make sure no one was hiding in another room while he was cooking up his meth.

Charlotte and Todd looked over at the house, and they could see Hernández peeking out from the slits in the newspapers he had pasted in the cracked windows.

Even now, said Todd, *he's for sure cooking up some stuff.*

Let's go, said Charlotte, and none of those two noticed that Sarah started walking across the field to the dying tree and the boy.

Who are you?

I'm Danny.

I'm Sarah.

You a new girl?

Fourteen. Is that new enough?

I mean, I haven't seen you before.

How do you know?

I've seen all the girls around here that look like you.

What do I look like?

You know.

No, I don't.

You're Filipina.

You Mexican?

See seenyor.

You live here in this town?

All my life.

You ever been out?

Went to El Paso once. Went to Juárez, too.

That where they killed all them women, yeah?

He shrugged his shoulders.

Well, they did.

She sat on a big rock, her pudgy legs jutting out of her skirt all knees.

Danny sat on a rock too.

What is there to do around here?

This.

She looked around at the field and saw he was right, that was all there was to do around here, and that was exactly what they were doing.

There's not even a movie theater in town, is there?

Used to be.

They were sitting opposite each other and the way the sun was hot on her lap and her white tennis shoes he imagined the light was a bowl of popcorn and he felt happy.

I guess you heard about that girl that was murdered.

Danny nodded.

You know her?

Danny nodded. He started to remember something about me, but he didn't; what was the point of remembering? Why haunt your own self?

She stood up. He looked up at her, his eyes squinted, his hand before his forehead because the sun was right above her, and she didn't say anything. She pulled out her pack of Marlboro reds from the back of her skirt waist and opened the box and offered one to him.

Hey, we're going to that house over there to score some stuff, Charlotte called over. *Come on.*

Sarah looked at Danny, and he looked down at the dirt and grass and then he looked up at her. Their eyes caught, and then a white fly flew right between their gaze and they followed it with all four of their eyes and then it disappeared in the sun and they looked at each other and laughed. She said to Charlotte, *I'll wait here with Danny.*

Hey, Danny. Nice to meet you, Charlotte said and waved at him from across the field.

And then, looking at Danny and Sarah sitting on rocks under the dead tree, Todd saw something. He saw a Doberman barking like crazy, like he wanted to get at them and tear them all to pieces, but then the dog ran to another part of the fence, like he wanted to single out Todd specifically, like somehow Danny and the others were safe, that the dog wanted him. He growled and barked at him, and Todd had a vision, saw himself being eaten by three Doberman Pinschers with snarling, bloody teeth, and he felt himself spinning around in a black-red swirl of blood and screams and he was spinning around and around and around in the field like it would never stop and he spun so fast he went back in time and saw the World War II GIs waving to the girls on the platform of the train depot, but it wasn't like he had seen before, because now all the men and women were Mexicans and Filipinos, which made sense, since half the town was, and always has been, Mexican and Filipino, and those were the boys the town sent off to fight in wars. There were even some blacks back in the war days, families who had come to work on the railroad a generation earlier and who would leave two generations later. For all we know, The Michael Carver might have been named after a negro American.

I should probably stay too, Todd said.

Why? asked Charlotte.

That stupid kid, he said. *He don't need to be around that stuff.*

Then a big diesel truck got stuck at the dead-end part of Oak Street and was trying to back up to get back on the road and the hell out of town. The big truck driver man pulled on his horn and revved his engine in reverse leaving all kinds of noises and some black smoke twisting and dissipating all around the air like water snakes.

The Framer's Apprentice

The white boy tried to have a conversation with the Latina girl, but she seemed so distant, as if she were standing alone in a field. As he added up the invoice, she was looking out the window, across the rooftops of Lincoln Ave., into the swirling sunset. He watched her sunken cheeks, her high cheekbones and the dark hair hanging loose over her face. Her eyes were almost blue, or maybe they were green.

"Beautiful sunset," he said, handing her the invoice, but he was looking at her face, like it was art on a wall.

She puckered her lips, and her eyelashes blinked.

She grabbed the sheet of paper, stuffed it into her sweater pocket, grabbed the framed image wrapped in white, and turned away. Right when she thought she was safely out of the framer's shop, right when her hand reached for and touched the sticky doorknob, the boy said, "My name's Zachary."

He was standing behind the counter, framed by the door behind him, through which she could see into a room of wooden frames, thousands of them stacked along the walls.

"And?" she said.

"What's yours?" he asked.

He saw her black hair swaying as she swiftly walked down the sidewalk and out of view.

That night, as she lay in bed, she recalled him standing in the framer's shop, how his erect body made a perfect cross with the horizontal counter top. The picture she picked up for the priest that day was a copy of Veronese's *The Wedding at Cana*, when Jesus performed his first miracle. Zachary had showed it to her before he wrapped it up. Holding it in his arms, his sleeves rolled up. The drunken party in Galilee seemed almost bacchanalian, slaves pouring red wine from white cisterns into clay jugs, drunken guests climbing onto the rails of the house.

"Do you like it?" he had asked, and she blushed.

Now in bed, she rubbed her hands together, disgusted to think what had made that doorknob so sticky.

She began to hear that name everywhere, as if it were the most common name on earth, Zachary. She would hear it on TV, or shouted in the streets, or after mass. One time, when she was in line at the grocery store, she opened up a glossy Hollywood magazine and randomly turned to a page, some article about a soap opera actor named Zachary Boone. The headline read: *Zachary. He Loves You. You Love Him.*

One day, she had to take her grandmother downtown for some immigration work. The cold, severe buildings rose up so high they let in neither sun nor heat, and Angélica felt herself feeling woozy, like she might throw up. She put her grandmother on a bench at a bus stop and told her to stay there, that she would be right back. She ran into a McDonald's—just to go to the bathroom, not to get a Big Mac or a cheeseburger or a syrupy chocolate shake or anything even remotely sensual, indulgent or decadent—but just to use the bathroom. And there he was, Zachary, coming out of the restaurant.

"Angélica!" he said, quite surprised to see her. She looked at him as if she had seen the devil, and she swerved around him. He followed her down the shadowy hallway to the bathrooms. He said, "Angélica, don't you remember me? I'm the framer's apprentice."

She stayed in the bathroom for a long time, angry at him, as if he had planned the whole thing. She washed her hands in water so hot it made her flesh turn red, and then she dried them underneath the blower. Thankfully, he wasn't there when she got out, but when she picked up her grandmother and walked with her through the labyrinth of downtown buildings, she was nervous that he was following her.

The church had gotten a new computer and printer, and the monsignor was amazed at how easy it was to get high-resolution copies of the world's great paintings. It seemed as if he wanted all the images in the world to be framed. He kept sending Angélica to the framer's shop in West LA, a two-hour bus ride, but when the orders got too large for her to carry by herself, Zachary came by the church in the white company van, "Viola and Son Framers" written on the side.

She gave him *Venus, Cupid, Folly and Time, The Rising of Lazarus,* Millet's *The Angelus.* She handed him Impressionist landscapes, two versions of San Sebastián, and da Vinci's *Last Supper.* Sometimes she would have to spend hours with Zachary, so she could explain to him what the monsignor wanted, and Zachary wrote down the order and calculated the cost and asked her out to dinner.

She said, "No. That will be all."

Then she walked out of the room and went back to work in the church office.

One afternoon, she was at an intersection, and she was so absorbed in not thinking about him that she stepped onto the boulevard without looking. She heard screeching brakes, tires skidding, and she smelled burning rubber. She looked up and saw the Pepsi truck coming right at her, sliding across the intersection like a big block of ice. It missed her by inches and collided into the back of a van. The truck driver got out and started cursing her. The driver of the van (of course, of course, it was Zachary) got out too. He saw her standing there, frozen like Lot's wife, still looking at the spot from where the truck had been coming toward her. The truck driver was cursing at her, an archetypal truck driver in a white V-neck T-shirt with stained underarms. It looked as if he would hit her, so Zachary came to her rescue. He put his arm around her shoulder and led her to the sidewalk.

As for my father, he fell hard for my mother, not the first or second time he had seen her, not even when he saw her come out of McDonald's, but when she was being yelled at by the truck driver. Years later my father would wonder if that hairy man was an angel. He saw her standing like a statue in the street, next to that big, mean man, and he felt his heart skipping a beat, literally. He didn't consider that it might have been due to the massive amounts of coffee he had been drinking that very afternoon as he studied for his accounting final, and when I suggested it might have had something to do with it, I think he felt a little hurt, as if I should believe his story like a chapter from the Bible.

He said she was wearing a long white skirt, all the way down to her ankles, and a blouse of gauze-like material. She stood in the street, all points of view on her, everyone watching her stillness, people on the sidewalk, people in the windows of buses and buildings, people sitting in traffic in their cars, all of them looking at her, this earth angel, and she stood there in a daze, the material of her dress billowing around her ankles.

My mother's name was Angélica.

Yes, sometimes God writes reality like an amateur. He makes things so obvious, so theme-heavy: Angélica, Zachary's angel.

After that day he came around the church just to see her, and they sat next to each other on the pews of an empty nave. They walked in the garden, and Zachary pretended to make up a new language, and he spoke it to her, just sounds and rhythms, to which she rolled her eyes.

They walked the streets of her barrio. They ate taquitos standing up. They sat in parks and talked about ducks. "I like to watch ducks walk," he said. "It's cute."

"There's duck poop everywhere," she said, wiping it off her shoe onto the grass.

And finally, having accepted what she believed was God's will, my mother decided to sacrifice herself, even if she didn't know why. She didn't know what He was up to, but she had to have faith in His plan. God wanted her to marry my father.

Then one day, years later, when I was seven years old, less than a year before she would kill herself, she looked at me as if she had never seen me before. I was at the kitchen table, studying math, and she gasped. I wasn't really studying, I was making symbols up, creating my own math. She looked down on my work, at a letter I made up, and she put her hands over her mouth and said, "You're the reason! You're the one!"

"The one?" I asked, thinking I had done something wrong.

God was going use me in powerful ways. She told me that I was the reason she got married. She had done it all for me.

My father would tell me about the day she agreed to marry him. They were driving down Lincoln Ave. when she told him about it. They were going to the framer's shop, because my dad wanted to pick up his paycheck and take her to the movies. She turned to him and said, "I hate you for this." Apparently she had wanted to sound romantic, saying the opposite of what she had meant, but his heart sank fast, like he believed it.

"What did I do?" he said.

"You made me fall in love," she said, scooting closer on the seat to my father, like it was her duty.

The First Time He Heard Her Giggle

He would marry the geologist, kind of a geek, but a sexy geek, a geek with glasses and frizzy red hair held back with a yellow scrunchie. The first time he saw her in line at The Stream, she was wearing a tight green skirt and tennis shoes, and she was lanky and awkward and her glasses were nerdy-cute. He felt weird standing in line behind her, like he already knew her, as if he had time-traveled from the past and this girl before him he somehow knew was/is/would be his lifelong partner. He suspected she was sexy in spite of the visual evidence. She held a plastic tray with a salad and a diet soda, and he realized that she was the homely girl in those movies where in the end she takes off her glasses and becomes heartbreakingly beautiful. In the movies, it's only obvious, but in reality he may have been the only one who noticed her qualities. He looked around The Stream, trying to observe if others thought she was hot, but to everyone else she must have looked like a nerd, because they walked right by without looking, not a single turn of the head. He felt like a co-creator of her beauty.

After they had been dating for two months, she asked him to a formal event hosted by the Geological Society.

He showed up at her door with flowers, and the woman who answered was stunning. She wore a white evening gown, no glasses, and her hair was wavy and long. What perhaps captured his attention the most that evening was how comfortable she felt being beautiful. She was queen of the geeks.

They both got jobs as tenure-track professors at the same university, and neither of them wanted to consider whether the university pressured the physics department to hire him in order to get her, or if the geology department was pressured to hire her in order to get him. They were young, and they went into their careers positive that they could do something great in the world.

One day, when he was in his mid-forties, he opened his eyes from a nap. He was sitting in his university office, a flask of whiskey on his desk. He had their wedding picture in a frame, from back in the days when photographers still used film. Their puffy hair looked so 1980s, even though the picture was from the mid 90s. He looked around his office, at the walls lined by books, as if he were looking for another photograph, one that might have their baby girl. Near a window, there was a whiteboard with notes and equations sloppily written in black and red Sharpies, something about hidden dimensions, twisted and curled up like water snakes. Just then something occurred to him, a memory. He grabbed the flask, took a swig, and for the first time in his life, he remembered something new from that first time he had seen her in line at The Stream.

She wore a tight green skirt and tennis shoes, and her feet looked so big. He wanted to say something to her, and the first thing he could think of was, Excuse me. When she turned around, he asked, Is there anything good here? He had meant the cafeteria, a bad opening line, and he indicated with his eyes his tray with a plate of wet lasagna and hers with a salad of yellowing lettuce and grated cheddar cheese.

She didn't know if he was talking about the cafeteria or if he was talking about the university, so she shrugged her shoulders and smiled. He realized she didn't know on what level he was speaking, so he answered his own question. In The Stream, I think the lasagna is edible, he said.

Oh. I thought that maybe you meant . . . In that case I would have to say that the salad is pretty good.

But it's iceberg lettuce. It has no nutritional value.

She shrugged her shoulders as if to say, *So what?*

I'll tell you what, he said, sounding very confident, like a salesman, let's take this to the next level.

This? What *This?*

This conversation. What's good about the university?

Oh, that's easy. The Geology Department. It's one of the best. She placed her tray on the counter and the cashier started adding up her stuff on the register. That was what he remembered for the first time in his life, that she also had an apple on the tray.

You're in Geology? he asked, looking at the apple, as if it were a nemesis that had appeared from a parallel universe.

She nodded her head.

He felt a pain in his stomach. He left The Stream but he wasn't at the university in his office, he was in his current home, walking down a hallway lined with photographs he didn't look at because they were familiar and painful. He wondered where the geologist might be, and why was he walking down the hallway? Where was he walking to? He looked at his hands, wrinkled and bluish with veins, and he wondered how old he was. Maybe he had gotten out of bed to get something for his stomach, which was rumbling, as if he had diarrhea. He was walking to the kitchen. It must have been early Sunday morning because everything was so quiet. He walked down the hall, saw her in another room tending some plants. She was clipping leaves, cooing a Wandering Jew with, It's okay. Just a little haircut.

Her hair seemed darker, not so much red, almost black.

Hey, he said, and she turned around but it wasn't her. It was a teenage girl.

Hi, she said, happy to see him. Someone's obviously feeling better.

Who are you? he asked.

Oh, Daddy!

He was peeking into the doors of a lecture hall, at the entrance, and some woman was giving a lecture at the podium, but it was in French. He looked for his girl-friend, and he found her sitting in one of the front rows, frizzy red hair, glasses, pushing them up her nose as she took notes. She was rapt by the lecture, as was everyone else it seemed, but he had no idea what the speaker was saying. He only knew three languages, pocho Spanish, English and the language of nature.

He closed the door and waited in the lobby.

People streamed out of the lecture hall, and he was waiting for her, leaning against a wall, arms crossed like James Dean. She smiled to see him.

He remembered that they had been dating for about a month, and it was getting serious. She kissed him and said, I want to buy her book. Will you wait in line with me?

Sure, he said. It must have been a good lecture.

She's a genius, she said. She pushed her glasses up her nose. Her work on plate tectonics will change the way we think of the earth.

Why did she give her lecture in French? I couldn't follow it.

I could help you learn French.

The language of nature, he said. That's all I understand.

What's that? she asked.

Math, of course.

When they got back to her apartment, she said, Okay. If it's so much the language of nature, speak to me in math while we're making love.

He watched her unzip the back of her skirt and step out of it. They took off their underwear. They submerged their bodies into each other and onto the bed, and they kissed and touched and he began reciting equations—a song of songs, a stream of numbers and letters—what most closely described what he felt when they were making love, the Big Bang. He timed it so the equation of the creation of the universe ended with the ultimate explosion in their loins. Afterwards, sweaty and more in love than ever, he told her what he had been saying in math, and she giggled. The second time in his life he would hear her giggle.

The first time she was in line at The Stream. She had just finished paying and was walking away with her tray when he yelled, Hey, Geology! Wait up.

He paid for his lasagna and ran over to where she stood holding her tray.

I just wanted to say that I like the way you push your glasses up your nose.

Oh, yeah?

It's . . . uh . . . kind of hot, he said.

Is that supposed to make me blush? she asked, trying to sound street smart, like she had heard it all, but it was like she couldn't help herself. She blushed and let out a giggle.

The Spiders
(a koan . . . kind of)

The old man didn't notice that hanging off the ceiling above him was a deadly spider. He was blind, and he sat at his table before a bowl of soup. It was still steaming, and he leaned over the bowl, vapors rising to his nose. He held a pair of chopsticks in his right hand, clicking them together with anticipation. His room was small with no windows, and at night he slept on a mat. Stacks of books and scrolls, things he had wanted to read before he had lost his sight, surrounded the wobbly table where he sat.

It seemed as if the spider was looking down into the bowl of soup.

The old man took his chopsticks and picked up something from the bowl, squeezed it a bit to test its density, and he knew it was some deep green leaves of bok choy. He lifted the leaves dripping with broth to his mouth, blew on them and ate them. They were delicious.

He mindfully put down the chopsticks on the table, knowing exactly where he had left them, and he picked up the bowl and drank some of the hot broth. He set it down, reached for his chopsticks, and at that very moment, the deadly spider on the ceiling lost its grasp and fell, floating down like a feather all the way into the bowl. He splashed down at the same time the blind man put his chopsticks into the broth and felt around for a wonton.

The spider, stunned from the heat of the soup, tried to swim for life to the edge of the bowl, but the chopsticks came after him like giant claws in a Japanese monster movie, and the sticks picked him up by his fat body, his legs desperately trying to break free.

The old man lightly squeezed the chopsticks to test the density of the wonton, which caused great pain for the spider, and it didn't feel right or normal to the man. He figured it was a bit overcooked, but he was hungry.

He brought the spider to his mouth.

It was said that one bite of that kind of spider would cause the victim to suffer immense pain for three days, until finally their bodies would give up and they would die. The landlady usually cleaned the old man's room to make sure it was safe from these deadly spiders, but the room hadn't been dusted and the cobwebs hadn't been removed in several weeks, because the lady's sick brother was staying with her, an alcoholic near death, who moaned day and night for more drink and the names of different women.

She still brought the blind man his meals, but taking care of her brother, she sometimes forgot, and today this bowl of soup was all she had brought him in three days. He was very hungry.

The spider fought to free himself from the sticks, his legs moving wildly, and at the moment the old man brought the deadly spider to his lips—one of the legs slightly brushing his nose—the landlady knocked on his door.

"Are you listening to me?" she said. "I'm afraid this is going to be your last meal. My dear brother needs the room. He's not going to get better, and even though he spent his life drinking and all the bad stuff that comes with it, he's still my brother."

The old man put the chopsticks back in the bowl, and the spider, relieved for a second chance at life, ran fast over the mounds of vegetables and wontons to escape from the bowl.

The old man knew nothing was certain but the fact of food, so he picked up the chopsticks again, determined to enjoy his last meal in the room he had lived in for three years.

He plunged the chopsticks to the very bottom of the bowl, and he picked up a bunch of noodles and pulled them out of the broth. They rose from the bottom of the bowl like a mountain growing from the water, a magic mountain, and the spider, still trying to fight its way out of the bowl, rose up on the snaky terrain of the noodles, eight legs trying to grasp solid ground.

The old man brought a bunch of noodles to his mouth, and the rest of them hung down all the way back into the bowl, and the spider climbed up the noodles toward the old man's chopsticks. The man bit into the gathering of noodles, sucking a slimy swirl of them into his mouth, releasing the bunch with his lips and teeth, until they fell back into the bowl, along with the spider, who splashed on his back into the broth. His frantic legs fluttered.

Meanwhile, a second deadly spider, the same kind as the first, crawled down from a wall, across the floor, up and down a stack of books, and up the legs of the table. He walked toward the bowl, as if drawn by the smell.

The old man loved the taste of the noodles, so salty, so delicious, so hot, and he mindfully put the chopsticks down on the table, lifted the soup bowl and brought it to his mouth to drink. The spider inside the bowl tried to swim up to the other rim so as not to end up in the old man's open mouth. The little creature had to use the man's teeth to push off from with three legs, and he swam up the bowl.

The other spider stepped onto the pair of chopsticks, and before he was even halfway across them, the chopsticks rose from the table into the air like beams on a high-rise construction sight, and the spider held on. The old man wanted a wonton, so he took the chopsticks and put them into the bowl, and the second spider, not wanting to plunge to his death, crawled up the chopsticks, ready to bite the old man's fingers for relief, one of his legs touching the hair on the old man's knuckle.

But right when the spider's sharp, venomous teeth reached the old man's hand, the chopsticks plunged a second time into the bowl and the spider slid down the slick wood. The old man grabbed a wonton in his chopsticks, or so he thought.

It was, of course, the first spider, caught in the pincers of the sticks, while the other spider was right above him on the sticks, hanging on for life. The old man lifted the sticks and brought them slowly, mindfully, to his mouth. He blew on it, the hair of both spiders waving like grass in the wind.

Right before he got the supposed wonton in his mouth—the spiders ready to bite his flesh—the landlady knocked again, loud, angry.

"You hurry up with that soup and go," she said. "I'm sorry, but he needs the bed!"

The old man put the chopsticks back into the bowl, and both of the deadly spiders took the chance to crawl out of the soup and up the side of the dish, where they rested on the rim.

The old man held his hands together and prayed for forgiveness, because he had been so divided in his heart that he was ignoring the gift of food, and even if he did have to find a place to live, right now he had delicious, hot soup.

He picked up the chopsticks, plunged them into the bowl and picked up a wonton.

The spiders watched him from the rim of the bowl. The old man blew on the wonton, and put it into his mouth.

It was so juicy, shrimp, pork, so delicious, so wet.

The Puppy

When the assassin got into the city, he bought a newspaper and checked the ads under "Pets."

He found exactly what he was looking for, "Black Lab/German Shepherd mix puppies, $50 dollars." It gave an address not a phone number. He threw his suitcase on the bed, opened it and took out his gun. He put it in the holster in the waist of his pants, closed the suitcase and left the room. In the lobby a busload of Japanese tourists were checking in, surrounded by a city of luggage, and the harried woman at the front desk, the one who had checked him in, looked over at him and smiled. She was Filipina, and she tilted her head, like she was trying to say something to him.

There were two puppies left, and although one of them might have been a lab/shepherd mix, the other clearly was not. The lab mix was jumping all over the assassin's ankles, like she wanted to be lifted and played with, while the little one, the mutt, sat curled up in the corner, looking frightened at everything. He was scraggly, not like his sister, who had a fine coat of black hair and tall legs. This one was twice as small, and he had ears so long they dragged on the ground.

The owner, a Mexican man, was shirtless, and he was chewing food as he talked, practically licking his lips. "Just give me 30," he said. He had a big belly and spoke with an accent. "She's the best one," he said of the excited puppy. "Una hembra."

The assassin couldn't keep his eyes off of the shy puppy, which must have smelled something, because he was sniffing around.

"Mucha vida en la hembra," the owner continued. "Mira," he said. He bent over a bag of dry dog food and pulled out a handful of nuggets and put them at the assassin's feet. The lab puppy quit jumping on the man and started to eat a chunk, and it was hard for her, but she was determined, so she nibbled and gnawed like a savage.

The assassin bent over and took a nugget and placed it right in front of the shy puppy, which sniffed the morsel, his floppy ears dragging on the floor, and then he stuck out his little tongue and licked it.

"Ay, that one? Give me 20."

"I'll take him," he said.

He named him Snorkel, because he was always sniffing, even as the man carried him to the car.

They went to the pet store, and the man put the puppy in the shopping cart, and pushed him around the place, a warehouse of smells and movement. Snorkel sat up and took it all in, watched the man as he pulled cans of puppy food from the shelves, and dual bowls for food and water. He waved a few toys in front of Snorkel, a stuffed elephant that squeaked, and a giraffe whose neck was made of rope. As they waited in line, the assassin held the giraffe in front of Snorkel. He sniffed it, licked it.

Snorkel followed the man all around the hotel room, to the window where the man stood staring out, to the desk in the corner, even to the toilet, curious about the sound his urine made as it streamed into the toilet bowl.

One day the man heard the puppy drinking. He had his head down in the water bowl, and his ears were so big that the ends of them floated. When he looked up at the man, licking his mouth, his ears were dripping.

His favorite toy was the giraffe, and his favorite game was tug of war. He pulled hard on the giraffe, baring his puppy fangs as he growled, trying to pull the giraffe his way, stiffening his back, his legs. The man let go, as if the dog was too strong, and he exclaimed, "Wow! You're so mighty!"

Snorkel dragged the giraffe away and took it to the corner of the room, curled up with it and chewed.

At night, the puppy slept on the bed, both of them curled up on different spots, and when the puppy needed to pee, the man sensed it, because he was a light sleeper and could feel the squirming. He carried him to the bathtub and waited while the puppy sniffed around, then looked up at the man, as if scared, as if he didn't know why he was in that white, hard terrain.

"Go pee pee," encouraged the man, and, when he did, the man made a big deal out of it, called him a good boy. He picked him up, kissed him. "I'm so proud of you!"

As he held him in his arm, he turned on the water in the tub and let it run for a few seconds. Then he turned it off and watched the water mix with the urine, the faint yellow liquid swirling and swirling around the drain, around and around until it went down and was gone.

Whenever he left the hotel, he took the puppy with him. He didn't bother with a leash, because Snorkel knew they were a pack of two, and he wanted nothing more than to be part of that pack. When the man let the puppy down on the sidewalk, or as they walked along the beach or in a park, the puppy moved his little legs as fast as he could to keep up with the man. The behavior of puppies was almost 100 percent predictable. There was little guessing as to how they would act, because their personalities were according to their species first and then their breed, and individuality played little part in it. The man knew the dog would follow him, and he also knew he wouldn't bark much. He knew he could take him anywhere. When he needed to go into places where they didn't allow pets, he held the puppy in his arms or hid him in his coat. He took most of his meals to go, and they ate in a park or on the beach, or sometimes in an outdoor café, Snorkel at his feet as he ate, chewing on a treat the man had given him.

One afternoon on his way across the hotel lobby, the Filipina girl stopped him. "How cute," she said. "I love your puppy!" she said.

He said nothing. Snorkel was in his arms.

She scratched him on the head. "What's his name?" she asked, looking now at the man, not the puppy.

He walked away.

"Okay," she said, with bruised dignity. She turned around and went back to work at the reception desk.

In the mornings Snorkel was crazy. He ran around the floor in circles and grabbed anything he could, the giraffe, the rubber elephant, towels, socks, the man's T-shirt, and he ran all around with it in his mouth.

But the morning was when the man liked to read. He read a Buddhist book in bed, not because he was Buddhist—he didn't believe in any spiritualism. He read it because he liked the language, the mindfulness. It was quiet, rhythmic. It gave order to his day.

Before he picked up the phone, he knew who it would be, because no number appeared on the screen, only a line of zeros, 000-000-0000.

"Can I speak to Mr. Marino?" the voice asked.

"Wrong number," said the man.

"Okay, sorry."

The line went dead.

The man took the puppy and left the hotel.

He waited by a pay phone outside a drugstore, and the puppy waited at his feet, sitting down, looking around as if everything was new. The phone rang and the man picked it up. He recognized the voice machine. It told him where the subject could be found, and how they wanted the job to look. Anyone can kill, but an assassin is a storyteller. Each work must be done with such detail that a narrative emerges, and under close exegesis of the case, every detail had to make sense.

The subject was a smalltime dealer, or used to be smalltime, but now he was into bigger things, which he couldn't handle because he was so stupid, so obvious, so bling. "He's a wigger," the voice said. "He's a white boy who thinks he's black."

After the call, the assassin walked to his car, the puppy following him. He opened the passenger door but the puppy was too small to jump onto the seat, so the man helped him up. They drove to a working-class neighborhood outside of the city. You could see the downtown buildings in the distance. He parked and sat in the car, where the old houses were big but had been split up into apartments. He could see crack dealers on some of the corners and a bunch of junkies sitting in alleys, standing in front of the liquor store. He spotted the subject coming out of a house, followed by some black kids. He was talking and gesturing, and the black kids listened to him, occasionally nodding. They were teenagers, but the white guy looked to be in his 30s.

He stood in front of an ostentatious Escalade, with gold-colored rims that sparkled, and he had so many chains around his neck he looked like a parody of a hip hop star.

When it was over, the man, back at the hotel, lay on the bed looking at the ceiling. He followed the lines in the plaster and paint and tried to find images within them, a face, a circus animal, a pirate, like he did when he was a kid, lying on his bed with the light on while the house was silent.

Then the image came to him. He saw himself walking on the beach somewhere in Mexico, with the Filipina woman who worked the front desk. They had a bunch of dogs, all kinds of dogs, following them, running, playing in the waves, chasing sticks, a whole pack of dogs, some of them old, walking slowly next to their masters, just content to be with them, some of the puppies chasing seagulls and pelicans. No matter how far the dogs ran ahead of them on the beach, or into the waves, all the man had to do was whistle and they came back. Together they went back to the condo. While the dogs slept in various spots around the house, the man and the Filipina sat on the balcony with a bottle of red wine watching the sunset.

"Come on, let's get out of here," he said to Snorkel.

He got up off the bed and began to pack. Snorkel thought it was a game and tried to bite whatever the man was putting into the suitcase. He tried to play tug of war with the man's shorts. Then he jumped into the suitcase and looked up at the man, his floppy ears hanging down like side curls. His tongue was hanging out.

He checked out of the hotel. He put Snorkel in the passenger's seat and then got into the car. He drove toward Highway One.

"Where do you wanna go, little fella?" he asked.

Snorkel looked out the window, happy, his tail wagging. The man rolled down the window, and Snorkel stuck out his head and let the wind run through his ears.

That night they pulled into a hotel by the coast, and the man put the puppy in a shopping bag with handles and took him to the room. The puppy thought it was a game, and when the man opened the bag and tipped it over on the bed, the puppy jumped out, ready to play some more.

"Tomorrow we'll run along the beach," the man said to Snorkel.

But that night another call came from 000-000-0000. The voice said, "Hank, is that you?"

"You got the wrong number I'm afraid."

"This isn't Hank in Visalia?"

"No, I'm in Santa Barbara. Sorry."

He hung up, and minutes later the second call came. "Is this the Walgreen's on Calle Real?"

"No it isn't. Sorry," he said and hung up.

Thirty minutes later he was standing outside of the Walgreen's on Calle Real in front of the public phone. It rang.

The next job was abroad, the mechanical voice informed him. He had to catch a flight to Mexico City.

The assassin remembered all the details, then he hung up.

He shook his head again and again, walking back to the car, where Snorkel waited in the front seat.

The next morning, before he checked out, he filled the bathtub. He got a towel and brought it to the bed where Snorkel was chewing on the rubber elephant. He looked up at the assassin.

He picked up the puppy with the towel and wrapped him in it like a burrito. Snorkel thought it was a game, and he bit at the man's hands with his little puppy teeth too small to even hurt, but the tighter the towel got around his body, the more scared he got. The assassin carried the bundle to the tub. He always did this so he wouldn't have to see their faces.

Snorkel didn't struggle much, as if he trusted his master, just like Felina, his first dog. He remembered how hard it was, how much he loved that dog, how much he felt for her personally, for her personality, even though he knew she was species first and then breed. He had singularized her, made her special, and every time after that when he got a puppy he promised himself he wouldn't do that, but almost every time he couldn't help it. Maybe that's why he always got another one.

He liked Snorkel a lot, remembered that time he was drinking from his water bowl and his ears were so big that they floated in the water. Now they had escaped from the towel and were floating in the tub.

The Things

When we fled, we didn't take our things with us, only what we could carry in our pockets or tucked away inside of our clothing. Trunks, suitcases and boxes were out of the question, unless we could somehow strap them on our backs and still be able to run, swim and climb, but even then, when we needed to blend in, we couldn't have a trunk attached to our back. This of course meant that we had to leave all our furniture behind, our domestic pets, statues of our heroes, our modes of transportation, porcelain dolls, stuffed bunnies, pots and pans, our favorite brooms.

We left behind some things that we still think about in the new world. One of us left a life-sized wooden bear that one of our ancestors had whittled with an axe and knife, and another one of us left a bureau, a writer's desk painted with bright colors, intricate images of angels and goats sketched on the drawers. Every decade or so, we would pull the bureau from the house and we'd get the most talented painters to touch it up so it always looked new.

Many of the items we left behind were easily replaceable in our new cities, that is, minus the sentimental value, a wicker chair with a red cushion, a collection of smoking pipes chewed at the tips, a wooden toy box with a baby bear painted on the side. However, what we longed for most were the objects that we singularized to be special above other things, not just telescopes powerful enough to see the stars, but *our* telescopes, *our* wardrobe closets, *our* bookshelves and tables and podiums and distilleries. A storyteller among us describes what a chair must have looked like without us there to sit in it, the chair alone facing a window that looked out onto the yard, our things strewn all over, a telescope half-buried in the dirt, a yellow wheelbarrow full of red clay pots, a ladder against the trunk of an apple tree.

But what we were able to bring with us, the small things, we were happy to still have, although today there is very little of it left. As will happen, we have seen much of our youth inundated with new cultural values and behavior. In order to experiment with drugs and alcohol or brand-name items that made individuals in our group individuals in another group, some sacrificed the things that were most valuable to us, an heirloom wedding ring, a gold watch on a chain. Our youth got jobs and apartments and cars and lived life as if we had been here for generations, forgetting our holidays and customs. Our national pride was reduced to decals of our flag placed on the back windows of our Hondas and Humvees. Our youth idioms varied only slightly from the popular culture's way of communicating, adding a few linguistic *isms* associated with our people. For example, in decades past, the black urban youth used to say, "That's the bomb!" to indicate strong approval, whereas our urban youth, those who forgot the old ways, would say, "We torched the village!" If we were to consider that phrase, we would recognize that a torched village (especially for us) is not positive or desirable.

Now there were few of our things left. Some of us decided we should gather some of them together and put them in a museum. We bought an abandoned tenement building, where the first wave of our people had settled into, in a section of the city that for two decades would become known as the diminutive of our native land, a once-thriving neighborhood between "Little Italy" and "Little Mexico."

In this museum, we wanted to display the things we had brought over with us, and we asked our families to donate our most prized possessions. We wanted the young to see that we had a proud past, worth preserving.

The call for things went better than we had expected, and we were shocked one morning when we opened the doors of the museum and saw hundreds of us holding arms full of stuff.

We had to pile things in the middle of what would be the main gallery, and for several days, as more and more people brought things, all we could do was stand in awe around them and try to imagine them in their places at home. We imagined an Egyptian cross nailed to a wooden door, a jeweled elephant near a window looking longingly at the rosebush outside. We imagined a king's crown next to a sword on an empty stage where our entertainers used to set up their spectacles. It was when we were still collecting things for the museum that something amazing happened. It will live in our memories forever. It has become part of our lore.

We were lined up outside, lines going all around the corner, carrying bags and boxes and wardrobe bags. Suddenly, an old woman walked up the front steps, hunched over, wearing a black skirt and scarf, and red knit gloves. She stepped into the museum holding nothing in her hands.

As she walked across, she stepped on some things, breaking a cigar box under her weight. Some of us were going to guide her back outside and tell her to come back when the museum was open. She wore a necklace on which hung tiny mirrors, and we could see ourselves getting closer to her. We were talking at her, asking her if she needed help, when she stopped us with a gesture of her palms. She spoke up, in the original language, words that none of us will ever forget.

She said she "had" something to give us. Our verb *to have* is confusing for many other linguistic traditions, because the first person doesn't exist for us, so although she meant "I have something," it would have to be literally translated as "We have something."

For the sake of narrative clarity, we have singularized the old lady, pulled her from the collective. *She* said it was something she forgot she had brought over. She said she had carried it across snowy mountains and asphalt roads and through forest after forest and city after city, but she had only recently found it again in a box in the attic. This, we were assured, would be the cornerstone of our museum. Show us, we told her.

She put one tiny arm into her skirt pocket, deep down, all the way to her elbow, and she felt around for it. Then she pulled out a cloth, black, faded, bound together by twine, and she proceeded to unwrap it. We were all so intrigued, wondering what it could be, and we started chanting words our people spoke in situations like these. She unraveled the object, and we felt that we would be transformed out of that brownstone building in the city, as if with each word of our chant we would rise higher and higher from our bodies, like spirits looking down on the living.

Then we got a glimpse of the object. It sat in the palms of her red-gloved hands, but it had been so long since we had seen such a thing, so ordinary back home, so long since we had thought about it, that our consciousness began to try and understand the object and convert it into contemporary concepts. Some of us saw a toy soldier. Some of us saw a letter opener. Some of us saw a silver coin, and one of us saw twelve wooden matches, but it was none of these things. We couldn't see what was in her palm because we had no memory of it. Maybe the oldest of us got a glimpse of it, and maybe we could hold it and pick it up if only for a moment, but the flash of recognition at first came to us all. We saw it, but its image was not contained in our understanding, so we didn't see it.

What if, thousands of years ago, a peasant came home to his family and unwrapped a thin, laptop computer, an Apple? How would anyone be able to conceive of it, to see it the way we would see it? What would they see? Some might see a monster, others a demon, an oracle, but they wouldn't see an Apple because they would have no room in their consciousness to perceive such a thing. The object would be so out of ordinary perception that it could disappear, or never appear in the first place. The family could look at the table and see empty space and think the man was crazy.

Even if we were to face a visible phenomenon beyond our understanding—a spirit, a demon, an angel—because such a thing cannot be conceived in our consciousness, we would have to represent it visually as something entirely different, a tree, a large rock, a bush blowing in the wind. Perhaps this is why when we are walking at night, we see a demon, but when we quickly turn to get a better look, all we see is a tree with branches reaching out to us.

So long had we been away from our homeland that the thing the old woman held in her red hands began to convert into light, and then it spun like a tiny star, and then *phht!*

It disappeared.

"You saw it?" she asked, weeping. "You saw it!"

We nodded, yes, we saw it, but all of us, later on, as we lay on our couches, a rag over our foreheads, looking at the cracks in our ceilings, tried to recall what it was we hadn't seen in so long.

But all we could remember was that in the palms of her hand was light, so distant it wasn't even light, but the memory of light, like when you wake from a dream and you forget the details right away and you see only a glow over a lost city. We try and try to remember it, but all we see is that glow, that waning light in the palms of the old woman's hands.

The Lady in the Plaza

"Art after Art goes out, and all is Night."
Alexander Pope

The violence would begin with her breasts. The artist wanted to make sure they were firm, so even though on the model they were quite frankly a little uneven, on the statue they would be perfectly perky. He stepped back to get a look at his work and sighed with desire. He hadn't even known her name, she was just some Indian girl in some village he had been passing through, and she was at the lake with the other women washing clothes. She had long black hair, as Indian as possible, and he surreptitiously stood behind a tree and watched her. He got a full frontal view. He was able to see through the wet white cloth to her brown chest. He saw that her breasts were uneven, one of her breasts larger than the other, one nipple lower than the other.

Now he stood before her statue in the plaza, and he marveled at how much he had improved the girl. Everything else as far as he could remember looked like her. It would stand forever in the middle of the plaza, in one of the federation's southern states, the most important city in that state, and even though he had seen her in another region, he hoped that someday she would come into the city and see her own image and recognize herself. The artist had little capacity to imagine his personal happiness—life was shit, he knew—so even in his fantasy of someday seeing her again, she was no longer a young girl, but a very old woman who would be stunned to see a likeness of herself as a girl. In his fantasy, she would make it her lifelong task to ask about the artist, and after years she would find him, old and dying of cancer on his deathbed. He would recognize her right away, and she him, and she would confess, I never forgot you that day by the river. The way you looked at me penetrated me to my soul. I always hoped you would come back.

Their hands would touch, and he would die.

When General Juárez asked him to build a great statue, the artist hoped his work could speak the words about her that he was never able to speak himself, and now, standing before the girl—she rose over him five times as tall—he knew he had done his greatest work ever, which was to be displayed in the city's center.

He had never liked to work while people were watching, so when he accepted the general's commission he had asked for privacy, and the general's men put a large tent around the plaza so the artist could work. He even slept on a cot inside the tent, and as afraid as he was of other men, he told the general's soldiers, when they showed up drunk and curious, that they couldn't come in. He almost pissed his pants in fear, but he stood up for his work, and they turned around and left him alone.

Now, standing before the finished work, he saw that she was beautiful. She was standing naked and proud. To make the general happy, in her hand, she held a rifle. And her face looked determined, like she would defend her country, her people. She was made of white stone as smooth as marble, but she was obviously an Indian. She had a large Indian nose and lips, and it wasn't hard to imagine her as brown.

He perfected the technique that made it look like she was looking right at you. No matter where you stood in the plaza, as long as you faced her, she looked right at you. My love, he said, and he looked around to make sure he was alone, and he couldn't help himself. He embraced her, felt the cold hardness of her belly on his face, and he mumbled words of love.

On the day of the unveiling, the general's men set up chairs and a bandstand in the plaza. It would be a big deal, because it would show that the general's city, Ciudad Gemelo, was as great as any other in the world. Never mind that it was such a violent city, there were daily murders, and mothers never let their daughters walk alone. The general himself was a violent man, and after the war in which he had performed so well for the federation, the powers in the capital gave him Ciudad Gemelo. He still carried a pistol on one side and a sword on the other, and there were rumors that he sometimes pulled out his gun and put a bullet in someone's head.

The general had told the artist what he had wanted. He wanted a national icon, a woman like America's Lady Liberty, like France's La Madeleine, like Fontana di Nettuno in Rome, something that would put his city on the same level as other great world cities. He was short, so the artist had to lean down to reach the general, who pulled him close by the collar so that their faces were about an inch from each other. The general smiled and said, No religious bullshit, understand? The artist nodded that he understood. He could smell sausage and coffee on the general's breath. You better do this right, yes? he said. He pinched the artist's cheek so that it hurt, and then he laughed and slapped him friendly-bully-like three times on the face.

He had wanted to create a safer work of art, a European-looking woman holding up a rifle, the gown hanging from her shoulder exposing a single breast, but he couldn't deny where the work itself seemed to want to go. A stone had its own spirit, its own élan, and his job was to chip away the pieces that weren't supposed to be there, revealing what had been there all along. Even as he chipped away more stone, he knew that what he was releasing was not what the general had wanted, but he couldn't help himself. He couldn't make a false image, and he hoped that the general would see the inevitability of it and would put aside any image he had before. The artist hoped he would like it, and he hoped the art (and it *was* art) would make the general civilized enough not to kill him, although the idea of dying for art's sake did secretly appeal to him.

On the day of the unveiling, a thirty-piece brass band set up, tubas, French horns, saxophones, and there were streamers and national flags and state banners with the general's picture on them. The artist was nervous. Even as he stood in the stands in a seat of honor, he was nervous that it would all end badly.

When the announcer introduced the general, people cheered, holding banners that had his name, and his soldiers stood around the audience, just to make sure they cheered. Even the artist held up his banner and squeaked, ¡Ajúa!

The general made a speech about himself and all his triumphs and about his great city. Finally, when he got to the part about the statue, he told the crowd he had chosen the best artist in the federation, coming all the way from the capital for this commission, and as the artist sat and heard what the general said about him, all the people looked at him and cheered and he blushed. He thought, This is what it's all about. A little appreciation. That's all we want.

My people, said the general. With no more further ado, here she is! The symbol of our great city! He waved his arms and at that moment the soldiers pulled the ropes on both sides of the tent and it fell down revealing the lady of the lake.

The sun was so bright that she shone like an angel, that white stone so glaring some people had to cover their eyes. The general stood there, not moving, looking up at the statue. The artist couldn't see his expression, just his back, his shoulders, his arms. It was so quiet in the plaza that they could hear a distant caw of birds.

The general's back seemed to grow tenser each moment. He walked closer to the statue. He looked up at her, his head came to about where her pubis was. When he turned around there was no doubt he was angry. Where is that fucking artist?! he yelled. Everyone in the bleachers looked at the artist.

What is this shit? he asked.

The artist stood up, hands before his chest, and he said, Do you like it?

This is a stupid whore! I wanted a woman of dignity. Dignity! Where is the dignity in this?

Well . . . .

The general climbed up on the base of the statue and pulled out his sword, and in one smooth motion he chopped at her breast, and a piece fell off and into his hand. He threw it to his soldiers, and they all reached to catch it like the garter belt at a wedding, and the one that got it held it up and the others cheered. Men in the audience were laughing, and the women were silent.

She looks like a prostitute, he yelled.

The soldier who got the chunk held it up and said, ¡Mamacita! and all the men laughed as he sucked on it and pretended to be getting milk. The general cut off other chunks, which fell into his hand, and he threw them into the bleachers. The women recoiled, but the men tried to catch the parts, and they cheered each other when someone got a piece of her. The general pulled out his pistol and aimed it at the belly of the statue. Women in the audience got up to leave.

After the violence, the general went to him. He grabbed him by the cheeks and pulled him down to his own face. You're lucky we don't do this to you, you son of a whore!

I'm sorry, General!

He told the artist that tomorrow he will start again, but this time no tent around it. To hell with your artistic ideas, he said. It better be what I want.

He put a gun to the artist's head and said, Understand?

The artist nodded, tears falling from his eyes.

He stayed in a hotel that night, right on the plaza, and all night long the city's men gathered around the statue drinking, pulling away her parts, her eyes looking into his window right at him. That was what disturbed him the most, that she kept staring at him, and he thought, Curses on a stupid artist's trick.

The men kept up their drunken fun even after the strong summer rain came and the dust from the white stone mixed with the dirt and swirled around in puddles at their feet and the black water rose to their ankles. Some men climbed up her body, and one boy stuck his head in her butt and waved around his arms as if he were stuck in there.

Below his window, the artist saw that some of the city's women were gathering. They were watching the men in horror, and all night long the artist kept hearing their voices, ¡Ni una más!, the women witnessing the violence his "artistic" image had caused.

Part V

Hotel Juárez

". . . but they just can't kill the beast."

Avenida Juárez

The professor passed by a large window of a restaurant—whole chickens roasting on Ferris-wheel spits, the birds slowly moving up and down and around—and he saw two men sharing a plate of tacos, pulling meat from the carcass. One of the men was drinking an orange Fanta in a bottle. At the counter, the girl who worked there was counting money. She had ponytails.

The professor jumped off the curb and walked across the street and onto the other curb. The sidewalks were broken and uneven, like ridges of an accordion, and some of the holes in the ground were black. In the puddles, he could see his own reflection looking down, and the look of desperate want in his eyes surprised him, because he thought he was at peace, taking a quiet Sabbath stroll. Young men against walls, watching him walk by told him with their eyes that they could get him anything he wanted, anything, just follow them onto the side street, but he knew not to trust them. If he was looking for something, he'd be better off to ask a "parkero," a man who held a red rag and waved it around like a lasso, guiding cars into available spots. While you were gone, he watched your car, sometimes washed it, and he worked for tips, but in between cars, he could take you anywhere, could get you whatever the city had to offer.

He knew taxi drivers could get him anything, too, those barking men always standing around in front of old model American cars painted green and white.

"¿Taxi, amigo? ¿Chicas? You want girls?"

"No, gracias," he said, as he crossed another street. He felt strong today, like he really wanted to use his body, wanted to walk all day, it didn't matter where, because paths were made by walking.

16 de Septiembre

The faster he walked, the faster the city seemed to wiggle like camera shake. The sidewalks were crowded, people streaming by him, pushing against him, so close he could smell their bodies. Cars on the streets honked and swerved around old city buses painted faded colors. He stepped onto the street to walk faster than the stream of people, and he almost got run over by a boy on a bicycle, the front basket full of bread. He walked faster, almost holding his breath, and he imagined that things around him began to move faster, too—the camera in his mind's eye sped up so fast that he saw blurs of moving color—and he reached the plaza and stopped.

Across the expanse, the cathedral jiggled in the smoggy air like a mirage.

He crossed the street, and the plaza exploded.

Vendors yelled out. Men sat at the benches or on the rails around the garden. A gazebo in the center of the plaza had a bandstand, and some children were running up and down the stairs like angels on Jacob's ladder. A statue of the famous comedian Cantiflas, a Juárez native, stood life-sized in some grass. Some Aztec dancers were out today, two dark, half-naked men, burning sage in a clay cup and dancing in circles and chanting. A crowd of people gathered around to watch. There were raised flowerbeds lined by stone barriers, which served as benches. The professor bought a hot cup of steaming corn, and he found a spot next to an old man. He sat down. He closed his eyes and wanted to be in Mexico. People often said that Juárez wasn't really Mexico, that it was too corrupted by the US, too close to Uncle Sam to be authentic, and they would speak with nostalgia about their summer in Oaxaca or their two-week stay in San Miguel de Allende. *Now that's Mexico,* they'd say, *The Real Mexico,* and the professor thought, Bullshit. Only a gringo would say that Juárez wasn't really Mexico. He opened his eyes, and sure enough, he was in Mexico.

The Best Tortas, Ever!

He ate fast, realizing after the first mouth full of hot, salty kernels how hungry he was. The old man next to him, who had a birthmark on his wrinkled neck—a big blotch of black skin—looked at the professor, nodded his head and laughed.

"It's very delicious," the professor told him in Spanish.

"It's good to enjoy your food," said the old man.

"I agree."

"Do you like tortas?" the old man asked.

"Yes, I like tortas."

The old man looked at him closely, in his eyes, examining him so minutely that the professor turned away.

"Yeah!" he said, laughing a hearty laugh. "You like tortas! I can tell!"

"Guilty," said the professor.

The old man leaned into him, as if he were about to tell a secret, and he said, "I know where you can get the best." He sat straight up, nodded his head, as if to say, "It's true." He took his fingertips, put them to his lips, and he kissed them. "The best."

"Where's that?"

"Just down there," he said, pointing to the other side of the plaza, across the street, where the mercado began. Crowds of people walked through the narrow passages, past booths where they sold pants, underwear, T-shirts, tools, CDs, DVDs, electronics. It was a giant outdoor market, not for tourists, but where locals shopped. At the entrance was a yellow dog, a stray, sniffing the air as if the smell of cooking meat fed his hunger.

"It's just on the other block. The best tortas you ever tasted. My favorite is the weenies." The old man rubbed his stomach, and the professor thought it was cute. "You like tortas, right?"

"I do," he admitted, looking at the dog across the street. He looked down into his Styrofoam cup of corn, seeing the few kernels sticking to the bottom, and he wished he could feed them to the dog.

Then an explosion went off, people clapping and whistling.

The Aztec dancers were spinning around and around so fast that all he could see were blurs like spinning tops, the feathers of their headdresses blurring the color of roses, the crowd getting more excited. Then they stopped spinning, and the crowd cheered. The two dancers were thin and fit, but the leader was the older one. He had long hair, a naked bronzed body, and now, as the professor looked more closely, he could see that the skin on his chest and stomach was loose, like the body of an old person. The dancer's muscles were defined, but the loose skin jiggled. His eyes were dark, with deep holes and wrinkles around them.

14

"I can take you there," said the old man, as if all this time he had been thinking of the best tortas in the city. "I'll show you how to get there." He made that gesture again of kissing his fingers. "The best. Come on, I'll show you."

"Sure," he said to the old man. "Show me the tortas." He stood up. "I'll even invite you to join me in one."

"That's very kind of you," said the old man. "Come on." He stood up and walked, and the professor followed.

Only then did he notice how tall the old man was, and not frail, but kind of taut, tall and lanky. He had tattoos all over his arms. He wore heavy steel-toed work boots and Ben Davis work pants, baggy and creased.

They walked through the mercado, some passages so thin that they had to push their way through.

"You're not from around here," said the old man.

"I live in El Paso," he said.

"No, that's not what I mean. You're not from El Paso."

"How can you tell?"

"Your accent."

"I'm from California," he said.

"Califas," said the old man. "Fresno. You know Fresno?" He spoke in English now.

"Sure, I know Fresno."

"I lived there for years," said the old man. "Lived in all those towns, Visalia, Merced. I worked in grapes and oranges."

"Why did you leave?" he asked. "Didn't you like it there?"

The old man stopped, looked at the professor and said, "You're joking, right? Why else? La migra."

He started walking again and the professor followed. His hands were huge, and they hung down his long arms all the way to his knees.

"Pinche migra finally caught up to me. They did raids every Tuesday morning in the apartments. Same time every week they went down the hallways asking to see papers, and if you didn't have them to show, they took you away. Everybody in our building knew this, even me, so all us sin papeles stayed away. ¿Entiendes? It was like a game. La migra knew they would only catch people so new they didn't know yet, and we knew they wouldn't catch us. It was like an unspoken truce. All you had to do was respect that every Tuesday morning they would pull up in their green vans and all you had to do was *not* be there. It was like a gentlemen's agreement. Everybody was doing their job. Everybody was happy. But one time I forgot. I had been out all night long with my homies."

"Wait a minute. Your *what?*"

"My homies," he said.

He stopped walking again, and he faced the professor. Behind him rose a booth where they sold women's accessories, combs and brushes and hair pins, and the girl behind the booth looked bored.

The old man was about a foot taller than the professor, and he didn't look so old anymore. Maybe only in his forties. Maybe he was the same age as the professor. He pulled at the skin on his neck, the black spot, and when it was stretched out like a canvas, the professor could see that it was a tattoo of the number 14.

"Norteño," said the professor.

"That's right." He started walking again. "So it was a Tuesday, just about the time la migra visits our building, pero me olvidé."

The girl at the booth watched the men walk away, bored, as if there was nothing else for her to do.

"It's hard to picture you as a gang member."

"What? You think they're all little kids with attitudes? It's much more organized than you think."

"No, I understand that. My brother . . . It's just . . ." He wanted to say, "You seemed like such a nice old man. Now you're a little intimidating," but he said nothing else. He just followed, and when the man turned the corner onto a narrow street lined by shabby bars, where plump prostitutes sat on stools at the entrances, he just followed.

"We're almost there," said the man. "How much do you want?"

"What do you mean?"

"For fourteen years I lived in Califas. The first seven years I worked in the fields. And what kind of work do you do? Let me guess: a journalist?"

"I'm a professor."

"Really? Of what?"

"Literature. Poetry, mostly." He wasn't sure if he should say that he once had a book of poems published. "I write too," he said.

"A writer, huh? I could tell you stories. My name's Paco," he said. He held out his hand, and he gave a Chicano-style handshake. "And you are?"

"Joseph," said the professor. "But you can call me Joe."

"Come on, Joe. We're almost there. The man led him into an alley, quite narrow, and no one else was around. "How much do you want, Joe?"

"What do you mean?'

"Come on, I don't fuck around. Give me the money. How much you want?"

"Of what?"

"Don't fuck with me," he said, threateningly. "You know I wasn't talking about fucking tortas."

Piedra

They were tiny white rocks wrapped in plastic. He found himself with about seven of them, in the palm of his hand, like uncut diamonds.

The old man/gang banger/drug dealer said, "It's good shit. I'm always there at the plaza. Every day, okay?"

Then he walked away, disappearing into a narrow passage between two buildings.

Joseph stuffed the rocks into his pants pocket, turned around, and found himself in a hot cement field, walled on one side by yellow buildings with the paint chipping off, piles of it on the ground like yellow fish scales. It was too hot, and there was nobody around except for a mangy dog on the other side of the cement field, standing there looking at him.

"Go away," he yelled to the dog with tentative authority. The mutt just stood there staring. He didn't wag his tail, nor did he have it between his legs, he didn't look happy or sad, he just stared. He must have been hot under the sun. His tongue was hanging out, and he was breathing hard. It was a yellow dog.

There was a narrow street lined by houses and beat-up American cars. He looked down to the vanishing point, and it was too blurry to see what was ahead, but he was sure that was the way they had come.

He found himself walking fast down that street, which was weirdly empty, not a person in sight, but he heard footsteps behind him. He thought he saw a shadow rising up the wall. He turned around, but he saw no one, just that same yellow dog, walking with him. Its fur was disheveled, sticking out in all directions as if he used gel.

Joseph stepped off the curb and into an intersection. All of the streets were narrow, and the concrete was broken up in chunks, and one of the roads was unpaved, just rubble. Some of the buildings were destroyed, the debris piled up in small hills. He passed some two-story tenements painted in faded pastels, most of the windows boarded up. When he crossed another street, he noticed some mountains in the distance, his mountains, El Paso, and his house was right at the foot of it, underneath the night-time El Paso star. He wished he were back home. His walk this day had started there.

Then it hit him.

He froze.

The drug wars.

That's why so many houses were abandoned and why everything looked like a war zone, because it *was* a war zone. Juárez had always been dangerous. First there were the hundreds of murdered women, girls who worked in factories, and now there were the drug wars. Of course, he knew this before crossing the border, but he always crossed, because he refused to be denied Mexico when he lived so close to it; Mexico, so far from God and so close to his front door.

When he crossed over into Juárez, all he usually did was stay in the plaza, which was more or less safe. He'd have a cup of elote, maybe sit in the cathedral for a bit and then head back home, but this time he had gotten distracted by a nice old man who turned out to be a gang banger, and he had those little white rocks stuffed at the bottom of his pocket.

He looked around. The street was quiet. Now, even the trees that he passed became sinister, Mexican alders reaching out their skinny arms to get him.

Hollister 22

And then, *thank God!*, it happened.

He found himself on that street again, where he had been walking earlier with the old man. The street gave way to the wide pedestrian walkway, which he knew led back to the mercado.

There were a bunch of people on the streets now, even those plump prostitutes standing before the bar entrances telling him to come inside. Some men were sleeping against the walls, and young, idle men stood around.

A man at the entrance of a bar—the door covered by curtains—yelled in English, "Girls? Are you looking for ladies?" Even though the professor was a Latino, a Chicano, they could always tell that he wasn't from Juárez.

At least there were a lot of people around, and he would be safe if he followed the street to the mercado, and if he crossed through the mercado he would be at the cathedral—ah, salvation!

He passed some boys, maybe 15, 16 years old, three of them. They were standing around a small tree dying in the middle of a cement circle. They were silent as he passed, watching him. One of them even elbowed another to point out the professor, as if to say, Míralo.

They were well-dressed for street kids, he thought, Hollister and Fubu T-shirts, designer jeans tight at the ankles, and they all wore bright, brand-new tennis shoes. They were all thin, almost feminine, and one of them, the tallest, wore a tight Hollister T-shirt with the number 22, the black fabric glinting like silk. This tall boy had his hair gelled, spiked at the top, and he wore Oakley sunglasses. Somehow, this kid had money, yet he looked like a street kid. He must have been the leader of the trio. He stood in the middle of them, his hand grasping the skinny tree as if he had an ostrich by the neck. They all watched the professor walk by.

Joseph wasn't sure if he should nod hello, because they were clearly watching him, and he thought that they would say something to him as he passed. Maybe they thought they knew him from somewhere. Maybe they were assassins. The woman who cleaned his house had told him that young men in the city knock off people for the cartels for a hundred bucks a head.

Suddenly, as if the yellow dog wanted to make a statement about loyalty, he ran up to the professor and walked right next to him, as if they were a pack of two. The professor wished he had something to feed the dog, and he looked around for a food booth. He could see that he was approaching what must have been the street right before the mercado, because it was wider and even busier with people, and there were food booths, a bunch of booths selling tortas and tacos and bowls of guisado and mole. Ladies had set up their own little tables and put on burners and pots. They put out folding tables and folding chairs. The yellow dog seemed to perk up with the smell, and you could tell he was happy, as if he knew the professor was going to feed him.

The food smelled good.

He stopped at one of the torta booths and ordered one with weenies. The lady served it wrapped in a paper towel on a paper plate.

He held out his hand full of dollar bills, about seven of them and indicated to the lady to take whatever she wanted, let her decide what price he should pay.

She took out two of the dollars and thanked him.

He took an extra dollar and handed it to her and said, "Gracias."

"Dios te bendiga," she said.

He took the torta and walked out of the lady's sight. It smelled good. He walked to the wall of a building, and he squatted down. The dog was excited and walked closer, a big smile on his face, his tail wagging. The professor couldn't help it. He took a big bite from the torta. It was delicious, moist and creamy. It was one of the best tortas he had ever tasted. He put the paper plate on the ground, and the dog looked at him with thankful eyes and then gobbled up the torta. He even ate the radish and licked the paper plate. Then he looked up at the professor, as if to ask for more.

Another dog started following him too, taking the third position. When he tried to get too close to the man, the yellow dog growled at him, bared his teeth, and even snapped at him, until the other dog fell in behind.

3 Stupid Dogs

He was getting close to the mercado, he knew, because he was passing booths where they sold sundry items, clothes, CDs, socks and underwear. There were candy stores and toy stores and butchers and tortillerías. There were ambulant vendors as well. An old man carried a box of triple-A batteries, and he yelled with a slight Mexico City accent, "Baterías diez pesos. Diez pesos. Nada más."

At a booth, the professor bought a bottle of water and a bag of potato chips. He walked a little while longer and found the mouth of the mercado. It was bustling with people. He sat on a bench against a wall, and he drank the water. He fed the chips to the dogs, feeding first the yellow one, but throwing some pieces to the new dog. He could see by her rubbery nipples that *it* was a she. She was much smaller, all black, rat-like ears. Her eyes were popped out like an iguana, making her look kind of dorky. She gratefully gobbled up the chips.

The professor looked up and noticed the three boys, the one in the Hollister 22 T-shirt walking in the lead. They noticed that he noticed them, tried to pretend that they were strolling around the market. The boy in the Hollister T-shirt stood by a vendor who sold soccer jerseys, and he pretended to be examining them for quality, baby blue Argentina, deep green Mexico. He kept peeking over at the professor.

"Come," he said to the dogs, walking into the mercado, which he hoped would take him back to the cathedral. He didn't want to turn around, but he couldn't *not* turn around. He saw them walking not far behind. He turned down another street busy with booths and vendors. He knew he was out of the boys' vision, at least for a while, so he ran fast, hoping to gain ground. He turned another corner, the two dogs running after him.

He could see the cathedral spirals peeking up over some buildings at the end of the street. He ran across the street, and he turned around, and the boys were running into the mouth of the street, after him. When they saw him looking, they stopped running and walked. They spread out, two of them staying on one side of the street, and the other one, the Hollister boy, crossing the street.

He was behind the cathedral when he noticed it.

It was a beautiful old building, colonial style, and it housed an art school and a bookstore. He went inside the bookstore, hoping he had lost the guys. He could stay in there until he knew it was safe. Then he would run across the street around the cathedral and into the main plaza with the Aztec dancers and the statue of Cantiflas. He would be safe there.

The bookstore clerk was one of those dressed-in-black intellectual kids, probably a university student. She was sitting behind the counter reading a book, and she had short brown hair and wire-framed glasses. The professor pretended to be looking at books, pulling them out and putting them back in without even registering the titles. He was thinking of those boys, certain that they were looking for him outside, hoping that they would keep going, thinking he was way ahead of them.

He glanced at the door, and he almost shit when he saw what was out there.

Two stupid dogs.

They sat in the doorway, waiting for him, as if they somehow knew they couldn't come inside the store. The three guys would walk by and see the dogs, and he'd be caught. He looked at the young woman behind the counter, so engrossed in her book. She was reading Schopenhauer, *El mundo como voluntad y representación*.

He wondered if he should ask her to call the police, and he could say he was being followed and he needed an escort to the border. But the police couldn't do anything for him, not with a drug war going on. They were probably too scared to go out by themselves on insignificant calls, and the Mexican army wasn't going to roll up with their rifles and military trucks and help him out. There were multiple murders every day, mutilated bodies found in alleys and doorways, stuffed in plastic trash bags or the trunks of cars. Last Friday, eleven top police officials had been murdered, execution style. What could the police do for him?

Then he noticed there was another dog outside, a little once-white dog with scars crusted all over his fur, three dogs now, as if two weren't enough to get attention. Even the people who walked by on the sidewalk looked curiously at the three dogs. They sat outside the bookstore, tails wagging like obedient pets. The yellow one was looking inside the store, and when he saw the professor, his mouth opened like he was happy, tongue hanging out.

Joseph started to pace very quickly back and forth, back and forth in the bookstore, wondering what he could do, back and forth, back and forth, willing some answer to come from somewhere. Then he stopped at a wall of books.

There it was.

Let the Dead Bury the Dead

He was standing in front of the poetry section, and there on the shelf right in front of his eyes, as if his will had bent the universe, was a book of poems by Baudelaire, *Las flores del mal,* bilingual edition, which is to say, *Les fleurs du mal.* He thumbed through the book and stopped on a poem about cats.

Ils cherchent le silence et l'horreur des ténèbres . . .

All he needed was a little daemonic inspiration. He needed a thick book, which could shield him from blows, and he could buy a sharp pen, his knife. He would get his shield and pen here at the bookstore, then he'd walk out of there as fast as he could to the cathedral, and if the three boys tried to get him, he would defend himself. He'd stick a pen in the neck of one, in the eye of another, block their wobbly punches with the book. Didn't he grow up in the barrio? Wasn't his own brother a banger? He knew how to defend himself.

But what book should he buy?

He didn't want to buy Baudelaire, because he already had multiple copies, and he needed something stronger, a hardback book.

Pablo Neruda?

The thickest Neruda they had was *Canto General,* which the professor, quite frankly, didn't think was that good. Why waste money on a book he would never want to read? When you buy a book you need to be excited, to walk out of the store pulling it from the bag, eager to read the first lines. You needed to feel as if you had done some great act of hope in buying a book. To buy a book and walk out of the store and not be eager to read it was a sad, sad thing.

Neruda wasn't the one, because the book he liked the most, *Residencia en la tierra*, he already had at home. Could Neftalí protect him anyway? He pulled out a thick volume of Gabriela Mistral, more Chilean love poetry, mostly about how she wished she were married and a mother. There was, of course, Amado Nervo, a Mexican from Michoacán, but it was a thin book of love poems, love too thin to block a punch. There was Octavio Paz's *Piedra del sol*, and Jorge Luis Borges' *La rosa profunda*, both of them far too thin. There was *Azul, Altazor, Ojos de otro mirar, La universidad desconocida*. There was a thick, hardback collection of Federico García Lorca poems, but buying Lorca at a new bookstore was like buying *Leaves of Grass* at Barnes and Noble. Who *didn't* have multiple editions at home?

It would have to be Gabriela Mistral. After all, that yearning she expressed in her poems, that obsession she had to be a mother or in a relationship with an elusive man wasn't about being a mother or being in a relationship with an elusive man, it was about being connected, feeling that heat emanating from beyond the fog. She accessed *that*, the portal he knew was there but had never gone through. Oh, he came close, sometimes getting glimpses into other places, falling into other dreams, but the moment would wear off, and he'd be back in his dull life, just getting through the days so the nights could fall on him again. That was what won her the Nobel Prize for literature, the first Latin American to win it: her ability to see, and hers was a feminine vision, which he could use in a place like Juárez. With all the dead souls of those murdered women becoming part of the very air and wind of the city, breathing in their dust-bones with each breath, he could use their protection. He needed a feminine deity. Maybe la Virgencita would notice his choice in books, and she would protect him. Maybe the Shekhinah, like a temple he would enter her, and everything would be all right.

He carried Gabriela Mistral to the counter. He saw a display of pens, standing upright in cups. He pulled them out one-by-one and tested their strength against his palm, stabbing it. He tried to determine if they were strong enough to go through a neck. If a pen seemed strong enough, he twirled it in his palm like he was a knife fighter, to get a sense of how it felt. The clerk was sitting high up behind the elevated counter, and she looked up from her book and looked down on the man spinning a pen, and she went back to reading.

Joseph found the thickest pen, made of metal, strong as a knife. He swirled it around like a dagger, and then he made a few quick jabs at the air, and he held up the Mistral book as if he were blocking an incoming strike, and then he jabbed the air two more times.

The clerk looked down again.

"¿Puedo ayudarte?"

The professor reached up and put the thick book and the strong pen on the counter and said, "¿Aceptan tarjetas?"

She nodded, put down the Schopenhauer and rang up the stuff. She did it very slowly, carefully, as if she were in no hurry, completely at peace with her task, her eyes bright with youth, and then she started to put them in a bag. The professor said he didn't need a bag, and he handed over his credit card.

Poet Warrior of the Night

The dogs must have sensed something from him, his attitude, his energy, because they were ready for war. They followed him like snarling beasts ready to attack his enemies. They bared their teeth to anyone who got too near the man, and a lot of people walking toward him or overtaking him on the sidewalk jumped back when they noticed the dogs. They walked further away, so there was a lot of space between them and the pack of dogs. The professor looked like he was ready to fight, he walked determined, the book in one hand and the pen in the other. He held the pen in his fist, as if he could bring it down hammer-style on someone's head, lodging it in their brain like an ice pick. He walked with the focus of an assassin, and he didn't so much look around for the boys as he simply glanced here and there, a wide peripheral vision.

In one corner of his eye, across the street, among the bustle of the market, he saw the boy in the Hollister 22 T-shirt, but he didn't see the other two boys. They must have been behind him, closing in on him.

He pictured the gray colors of the city coming alive in graphic-novel reality, saw his own figure with a cape walking into the dark city, saw himself writing poetry in rough taverns and getting into fights, saw the three sinister boys surround him with sticks and guns, saw himself spinning with knife and sword and chopping off their limbs, cartoon words popping in the air, *Bam!* and *Slash!,* and then, in the final frame, saw himself walking into the orange swirl of urban sunset.

The pen was not mightier than the sword, the pen *was* the sword. He stopped walking. He twirled the pen in his palm and then held it loosely, moving it around, as if ready to lunge in any direction. The boy in the Hollister 22 T-shirt knew he was being watched. He tried to act casual, unobserved, but he seemed to be trying to get the professor's attention, and when the professor looked in his eyes, the boy nodded his head, shrugged his shoulders, trying to say something to him.

22 looked across the street, to the left of the poet, near the bookstore where the other two boys were waiting. Joseph looked back and forth at them and the leader, twirling the pen in his hand. The boy gestured for Joseph to come across the street, follow him into the alley, but when the boy began to cross the street himself and come to the professor's side, the dogs growled at him. He stopped. He said with a nod of his head to the others boys, *Let's go.*

The professor saw that they were leaving, turning back.

322

After all this happened, after the professor had made it to the plaza in front of the cathedral, after he had bought hotdogs for all three of the dogs, after he pat on the head for one last time the yellow mutt, his favorite, after he decided it would be imprudent in today's climate to cross the border with crack in his pocket and decided instead to stay at a hotel he knew on a side street, Hotel Juárez, the sign and the entrance on the sidewalk, the rooms 200 pesos and up, less than 20 bucks, and after he got the skeleton key from the sleepy man at the front desk and walked down the dimly lit hallway, up the stairs to the third floor, to another hallway and past a number of numbered doors, dull lights on the ceiling making his shadow project weirdly on the walls, he came to his room number, 322. He knew how to use a skeleton key, knew the hotel, had been there many times before, and after he fumbled with the lock and let himself into the room, he admitted to himself that his imagination could have been transposed over his perceptions of the city. He often marveled at the human capacity for self-deceit.

Maybe the boys weren't even following him.

He closed the door to the room and made sure it was locked. The room was cold and smelled of old fabric, like a dead man's closet. He took out the rocks. He reached into his sock where he had put his glass pipe, and he pulled it out. He patted his pocket to make sure the lighter was there, and he headed for the bathroom. The first hit went through him like the color blue, and his skin tingled and buzzed, his bones jiggled, his spirit wiggled and his head expanded into a universe of voices and images.